W9-BJT-010

Praise for the
Royal Pains Series
by D. P. Lyle

"*Royal Pains* was a very enjoyable, light mystery. It had enough action [and] twists to keep you guessing and interested, and the characters are people you want to get to know better. . . . The medical scenes are well written in plain English. You will be entertained and learn some things you may not have known at the same time."   —*Suspense Magazine*

"This is the first television tie-in book I have read since I was a teenager, but if D. P. Lyle writes another, it will not be the last. . . . [T]here is a realism to the medical cases that comes from Lyle's long career in medicine. Pick the book up for your summer vacation even if you are only going as far as the wading pool in the backyard. It is a fun read!"

          —Kings River Life Magazine

"The relationship between Hank and Evan is fun, but Divya steals the spotlight. Her sense of humor is fun and intelligent, and she keeps the brothers on their toes. . . . [A] great summer read!"   —Fresh Fiction

"D.P. Lyle writes novels with TV tie-ins that are fun to read."   —Genre Go Round Reviews

"Lyle's work is well-known."   —Examiner.com

The *Royal Pains* Series

First, Do No Harm
Sick Rich

Royal Pains

Sick Rich

D. P. Lyle

DISCARDED BY
MEMPHIS PUBLIC LIBRARY

AN OBSIDIAN MYSTERY

OBSIDIAN
Published by New American Library, a division of
Penguin Group (USA) Inc., 375 Hudson Street,
New York, New York 10014, USA
Penguin Group (Canada), 90 Eglinton Avenue East, Suite 700, Toronto,
Ontario M4P 2Y3, Canada (a division of Pearson Penguin Canada Inc.)
Penguin Books Ltd., 80 Strand, London WC2R 0RL, England
Penguin Ireland, 25 St. Stephen's Green, Dublin 2,
Ireland (a division of Penguin Books Ltd.)
Penguin Group (Australia), 250 Camberwell Road, Camberwell, Victoria 3124,
Australia (a division of Pearson Australia Group Pty. Ltd.)
Penguin Books India Pvt. Ltd., 11 Community Centre, Panchsheel Park,
New Delhi - 110 017, India
Penguin Group (NZ), 67 Apollo Drive, Rosedale, Auckland 0632,
New Zealand (a division of Pearson New Zealand Ltd.)
Penguin Books (South Africa) (Pty.) Ltd., 24 Sturdee Avenue,
Rosebank, Johannesburg 2196, South Africa

Penguin Books Ltd., Registered Offices:
80 Strand, London WC2R 0RL, England

First published by Obsidian, an imprint of New American Library,
a division of Penguin Group (USA) Inc.

First Printing, January 2012
10 9 8 7 6 5 4 3 2 1

Copyright © Universal Studios Licensing LLC, 2012
All rights reserved

OBSIDIAN and logo are trademarks of Penguin Group (USA) Inc.

Printed in the United States of America

Without limiting the rights under copyright reserved above, no part of this
publication may be reproduced, stored in or introduced into a retrieval system, or transmitted, in any form, or by any means (electronic, mechanical,
photocopying, recording, or otherwise), without the prior written permission
of both the copyright owner and the above publisher of this book.

PUBLISHER'S NOTE
This is a work of fiction. Names, characters, places, and incidents either are the
product of the author's imagination or are used fictitiously, and any resem-
blance to actual persons, living or dead, business establishments, events, or
locales is entirely coincidental.

The publisher does not have any control over and does not assume any responsibility for author or third-party Web sites or their content.

If you purchased this book without a cover you should be aware that this book
is stolen property. It was reported as "unsold and destroyed" to the publisher
and neither the author nor the publisher has received any payment for this
"stripped book."

The scanning, uploading, and distribution of this book via the Internet or via
any other means without the permission of the publisher is illegal and punish-
able by law. Please purchase only authorized electronic editions, and do not
participate in or encourage electronic piracy of copyrighted materials. Your
support of the author's rights is appreciated.

ACKNOWLEDGMENTS

There are many people who made this book possible. I want to thank each of them.

My wonderful agent, Kimberley Cameron, of Kimberley Cameron and Associates.

My equally wonderful editor, Sandra Harding, who offered needed advice, criticism, and more than a few laughs along the way.

All the great folks at Penguin, including the publisher of New American Library, Kara Welsh.

Debbie Feiner, Patricia Masters, and Dr. James "the Hawk" Hawkins for lending their names to characters in this story.

A special thanks to James Fabrick, aka Jimmy Jam, aka Rat Boy, aka Blind Lemon Laguna Beach Fabrick, for his help with all things surfing.

The Hamptons:
Home Sweet Home

I'm Dr. Hank Lawson. I live in the Hamptons. Specifically, in the guesthouse at Shadow Pond, a sprawling estate owned by the mysterious Boris Kuester von Jurgens-Ratenicz. I call him simply Boris. The reason for this should be obvious.

The Hamptons weren't my first choice for a place to practice medicine. Nor the second, third, or any other number you wish to attach. In fact, they didn't even make the list. Weren't on my radar.

But life sometimes pushes you along a path you never considered. You're rolling along, have a great job, a fantastic fiancée, a glowing future. The sun is shining, the birds are singing, and violins provide your life's background music.

Until the train jumps the rails.

The music stops, the birds fly away, clouds darken

the sun, and your life looks like the rubble left behind by a hurricane or a tornado or a tsunami.

That's what happened to me.

I ran a very busy emergency department in a large and prestigious hospital. I was respected by my colleagues and admired by the hospital administration.

Until the train jumped the rails.

I should point out that an emergency room is a very dangerous place, perhaps second only to an aircraft carrier deck during flight operations. People die there all too often. Heart attacks, strokes, auto accidents, shootings and stabbings, runaway infections, and a long list of other maladies can do in even the healthiest among us. And on many occasions do so in short order. I had seen it all and weathered every storm.

Until the train jumped the rails.

My train wreck came in the form of a cardiac death. Not uncommon, but this time the patient was Mr. Clayton Gardner, a man worth billions, with a *B*, and as fate would have it the major donor to the hospital. I did nothing wrong and in fact nearly saved Mr. Gardner. The board felt otherwise, so I was fired and blackballed from the medical community. No job, no future, and no fiancée. Nicki, who I thought was the love of my life, bailed on me, too. She apparently decided that she needed to marry a real doc, not one who had been kicked to the curb.

The train had not only jumped the rails but had tumbled into a deep, uninhabited gorge.

Unable to deal appropriately with this mountain of

setbacks, I drank beer and watched weeks of reruns on TV. This actually made me feel better. Self-pity will do that. It can also be addicting. It hooked me and I settled nicely into a routine of doing nothing. Lucy, Ethel, and I became BFFs.

This stage of my life didn't last long, though. My brother, Evan, came to the rescue. Not that I went willingly, since I expected that whatever Evan planned would simply be another one of his harebrained schemes. When we were kids it seemed like he came up with two or three a week. Most were stupid and harmless, but a few got us in trouble. Nothing major, but we not infrequently found ourselves on the hot seat. Those are stories for another day. This time his idea was a trip to the Hamptons for Memorial Day weekend. The last thing I wanted to do. But Evan is persistent if nothing else. He also pointed out that I was becoming a slob and rapidly approaching flat broke.

What harm could a trip to the Hamptons do?

Maybe it would cheer me up?

Pushing my doubts on that point aside, I gave up the argument and said yes. My brother is very good at winning wars of attrition.

This little adventure into the wilds of the Hamptons led to a party at Shadow Pond, where I saved the life of one of the guests. A young woman who had inhaled a nasty pesticide while savoring a fragrant rose in Boris's massive garden.

As a way of saying thanks for my having aborted a medical, social, political, and financial disaster, Boris gave me a gold bar—yes, a real solid gold bar—and settled Evan and me into his guesthouse. He became my first patient.

From there my concierge practice grew. I'm not sure how, since I fought it for months, unconvinced that that type of medicine was right for me. But like breaking in a new pair of jeans, it soon became comfortable.

Now HankMed, the name Evan dreamed up for my practice, is very successful. It still consists of Evan, HankMed's self-anointed CFO, Divya Katdare, my self-hired physician assistant, and me. Our patient list has grown, we are solvent, even profitable, and once again the future looks bright.

I wish I could feel at ease with that, but the truth is I had my future blow up once before and I know it could happen again. Evan says I worry too much. That it's in my nature to do so. Divya cautiously agrees. I believe I'm a realist.

Chapter 1

"I think a pirate would be cool." Evan danced around the room, waving his arm as if brandishing a sword.

"You mean like Zorro?" Divya asked.

"Or Errol Flynn."

"Go with Zorro. The mask would be a definite improvement."

"Maybe an eye patch." Evan flattened his palm across his left eye. "Yeah, that would be cool."

"Did they have pirates in colonial America?" Divya asked. "Or was that later?"

"Sure they did. Blackbeard? Remember him?"

"Vaguely."

"He was ferocious. And studly."

"Neither being a word I'd use to describe you."

It was after sunset and the wedge of sky I could see through the windows darkened by the minute. I was sitting on the sofa, working on my laptop, listening to Evan and Divya argue. Their relationship seemed to be built around arguing—like two five-year-olds who had to share the same sandbox. This time the subject was costumes.

It didn't start that way but rather began while they were going over HankMed's finances. Divya suggested a new method for record keeping; Evan immediately resisted, saying he was the CFO and the one who should decide how the ledgers were kept. He was probably right, but I had to admit Divya's suggestion made sense. I was smart enough to stay out of it and let them lock horns. Now they had shifted to a discussion of costuming.

One of my patients, Nathan Zimmer, was throwing the must-be-seen-at Fourth of July party next weekend. It was the buzz of Hamptons society. The theme was 1776. Colonial attire. Evan couldn't decide what to wear. He had run through a dozen suggestions, Divya shooting down each one.

"Maybe you could go as Thomas Paine's long-lost cousin," Divya said.

"Thomas Paine? He was cool."

"Yes, and a royal pain. Not unlike you."

"Then you could go as King George. Another royal pain."

Divya laughed. "That was actually clever. For you."

Evan was undeterred. "Maybe I could be Ben Franklin. I love his little glasses."

"I'll avoid any reference to you flying a kite or getting electrocuted."

Evan finally gave up swashbuckling and sat down

at the kitchen table. Divya sat on the opposite side, laptop open, papers spread over the surface. The aroma of the lasagna Evan had made drifted from the oven.

My stomach growled. Apparently loudly.

"Somebody's hungry," Divya said.

"It's almost ready," Evan said. "As soon as Jill gets here I'll take it out of the oven."

Jill was Jill Casey, my on-and-off girlfriend and the administrator of Hamptons Heritage Hospital. She'd had a meeting that ended at seven and had just called saying she was on the way.

"I think you should quit fretting so much," Divya said. "It's just a costume."

"It's an important decision," Evan said.

"It's a costume," I said, immediately regretting jumping into the conversation. Some things are best left undisturbed.

"A CFO's costume," Evan said. "I have a reputation to uphold."

"What reputation might that be?" Divya asked.

"A CFO's costume needs to suggest wealth and success. Let people know that you're cool and someone important."

"That would be you," I said. "Cool and important."

"In his own head," Divya said. She tapped her pen on the tabletop. "And you think a pirate costume would suggest a wealthy and successful CFO?"

Evan stared at her, apparently speechless. Not a common condition for him.

Divya shrugged. "I suspect that nowadays a CFO

who plundered Wall Street might be considered a pirate, but I don't think that's the HankMed image we are going for."

"Why not go as a bookkeeper?" I asked. "It's a small step from accountant."

"There's a big difference." Evan was now getting worked up. "Accounting takes years of school."

I raised my hands. "Sorry."

Evan wasn't finished. "That would be like me calling you a physician assistant."

Divya raised an eyebrow. "And what exactly is wrong with that?"

"It's fine. For you but not for Hank."

Now Divya's jaw set. "Because I'm a woman?"

Evan hesitated, obviously measuring his words. Good idea. You never want to have Divya's ire aimed at you. She can melt you with a look and her words can incinerate.

"No, that's not what I meant," Evan said.

Divya waited. Me, too. Except I was holding my breath.

"I meant you didn't go to med school. Hank did. Most bookkeepers don't have degrees in accounting. I do."

I was impressed. All in all not a bad recovery.

"Either way, you already have accounting-slash-bookkeeping costumes," Divya said. "Go rummage through your closet."

"I don't think I have anything colonial."

Divya nodded. "Good point."

"What are you going to wear?" she asked me.

"Nothing."

"That's an interesting costume." She laughed. "Could get you arrested, though."

"What I meant is that I'll go as me."

"That way no one will recognize you," Evan said.

"That way I won't look like a fifth grader."

"Costume parties are fun," Evan said. "It's a chance to be a child again."

"My point exactly."

"What about you?" Evan asked Divya. "What are you going to wear?"

"I haven't decided."

"Maybe you should be an Indian princess?"

"In case you haven't noticed, I *am* an Indian princess."

"That's not the kind I was talking about."

"Are you saying I would make a good squaw?"

Evan stood and walked across the kitchen to the oven and pulled open the door. The aroma of the lasagna intensified. My stomach growled again. Evan removed the lasagna from the oven and placed it on the counter. "That needs to sit for about ten minutes and then we'll be ready to eat."

"You didn't answer my question," Divya said.

"I think you'd look great in one of those buckskin dresses with feathers in your hair. Maybe beaded moccasins, too."

Divya's glare launched a few arrows his way. "Perhaps you could go as a singing cowboy. A soprano if you don't watch out."

The door swung open and Jill came in.

"Sorry I'm late," Jill said. "I hope you didn't wait for me."

I closed my laptop and placed it on the table beside the sofa. "Not at all. We're waiting for the lasagna to cool. And I've had the pleasure of listening to Evan and Divya argue over costumes."

Jill placed the bottle of wine she'd brought on the table. "Any decisions made?"

"No," Divya said. "Evan isn't capable of making such decisions."

"That's not true," Evan said. "I just need to be sure the costume makes a statement."

"Statement?" Jill asked.

"Evan thinks his outfit should suggest power and wealth," I said. "Be CFOish."

Jill laughed. "Not sure what that would be."

"Something cool and professional," Evan said.

"Why not go as a bookkeeper?" Jill said.

Evan stared at her. "Do you and Hank compare notes?"

"What about you?" Divya asked Jill. "What are you going to wear?"

Jill sat next to me on the sofa. "It depends on Hank."

"He said he was going to wear nothing," Divya said.

Jill laughed. "That could get interesting."

"Actually I said I was going as myself," I said.

"That works for me," Jill said. "I've got so much going on right now that looking for a costume is the least of my worries."

Jill's project, and major headache for the past three months, was organizing the First Annual Hamptons Health and Fitness Fair at the high school. With the Fourth of July falling on Monday, the fair would be held on Saturday and Sunday—the second and third. It was not only to promote fitness and a healthy lifestyle but also to raise money for the high school, Hamptons Heritage Hospital, and Jill's community clinic.

"What's the latest?" I asked.

"We have all the tent booths set up around the track and football practice field. I saved HankMed a prime corner one. Near the entrance and directly across the field from the Hamptons Heritage booth."

The booths went for a thousand dollars each, but Jill had comped ours since we would be providing care to the attendees and those who would participate in all the athletic events she had planned.

"Thanks. We'll come by tomorrow and check it out."

"Looks like I'll be there all day, so anytime."

"What about the weather?" Divya asked. "Isn't it supposed to rain this week?"

Jill nodded. "They said maybe Wednesday or Thursday but the weekend will be clear."

"They're only right about half the time," Evan said. "You'd think they'd have weather prediction wired by now."

"It's not an exact science," I said.

"But there're a gazillion satellites that can see things all over the world. They should be able to tell us if it's going to rain or not."

"I think it's particularly unpredictable this year," I said. "Isn't this a La Niña year? Or is it El Niño? I can't keep those two straight."

"Me either," Jill said. "All I know is that the weather guy says it'll be clear this weekend."

"Either way, I'm sure everything will work out just fine," I said.

Evan tossed the Caesar salad he had made in a large wooden bowl. Divya cleared away her papers and laptop. Evan then carried the lasagna and the salad to the table, placing the former on a large quilted pad. Plates and flatware followed.

"Dinner is served," Evan said.

While we ate, the conversation turned to Evan's fund-raising. He had taken on the task of selling the booths and collecting donations from local businesses and the Hamptons' more wealthy citizens. A job that required schmoozing, something Evan held a PhD in.

"I honestly don't know how I could have pulled this off without Evan's help," Jill said. She looked at him and smiled. "He's been a real trouper."

Evan beamed and his chest expanded a few inches.

"He is a salesman," I said. "Annoying at times, but he can sell."

"When you have a good product, selling it is easy," Evan said.

"Well, you've done an incredible job."

"Almost all the booths are sold," Evan said. "Only two left. I have a couple of appointments tomorrow, so those should be filled then."

Evan went on to rattle off the names of some of the companies that had donated money, concluding by saying that they had already passed their goal.

"Really?" Divya asked.

Jill nodded. "Actually we're way over our goal. And that's not counting whatever comes in from Evan's charity walk on Sunday."

"I'm impressed," Divya said. She lifted her wineglass. "A toast to Evan."

We clinked glasses and took sips.

"What do you want?" Evan asked.

"Me?" Divya replied. "Why would you ask that?"

"You're being nice."

"I am nice."

"Just not to me."

"You rarely deserve it. This time you do."

There's nothing like the sounds of home.

The conversation returned to the health fair but unfortunately just as quickly flipped back to costuming. Not a subject that interested me a great deal but one that Evan had his teeth into. Obsession and Evan are old friends.

"I still like the idea of a swashbuckler," Evan said. "I can see myself as Blackbeard."

"Or perhaps the Scarlet Pimpernel," Divya said.

Jill laughed so hard she nearly choked. When she got her breath back she said, "You'd look so cute in tights."

"You guys are funny," Evan said. "I'm talking about a sword and an eye patch and maybe a jug of rum."

"Rum?" I asked. "That's what we need. Evan the drunk pirate."

"I wouldn't fill it with real rum. Maybe tea or lemonade."

"That's so Pimpernel," Divya said. "A lemonade-drinking swashbuckler. Mr. Flynn must be spinning in his grave."

"Maybe we should all visit that cool costume shop in East Hampton," Jill said. "They even supply the local theaters. They'd have all types of costumes."

"Good idea," I said. "Maybe then Evan can make a decision and I won't have to listen to this anymore."

"I wouldn't bet on that," Divya said.

I could almost see Evan's mental wheels turning and then the light behind his eyes snapped on.

"I've got it," he said. "A spy. I could go as a Revolutionary spy." He took a bite of lasagna, his head bobbing as he chewed. "That would be so cool. After all, Evan R. Lawson is a superspy." He held up his cell phone, aiming it at Divya.

Evan R. Lawson is a superspy.

Evan had once tricked Divya into saying a couple of nice things about him and had recorded her voice. He replayed them from time to time to annoy her. Like now.

"When are you going to delete that?" Divya asked.

"Probably never. I have another one if you'd rather hear that."

Evan R. Lawson is right.

Divya rolled her eyes. "You're impossible."

"But I have proof that you think I'm a superspy and that I'm right."

"It was an isolated incident punctuated by a moment of weakness."

"A spy might work," Jill said. "You could wear all black and a long trench coat."

"I could be like James Bond or Jason Bourne or George Smiley," Evan said.

"Maybe Inspector Clouseau," Divya said.

Evan R. Lawson is a superspy.

Evan looked at Divya. "And you could be Mata Hari."

"Just so I don't have to be Rosa Kleb."

"She did have cool shoes," Jill said. "Not cool-looking, but that little knife blade in the toe could come in handy. Every time I have to negotiate with a vendor."

"Ouch," I said.

"Some of them could use a swift kick."

Better them than me.

Chapter 2

The next morning Divya and I headed out to see patients—three follow-up visits and one new patient. Evan went along to drive the new HankMed van. We had had it a few months now and both Divya and I had to admit that it was cool. And it did help with making house calls.

We could carry more medications and equipment with us. The portable X-ray and ultrasound machines alone saved time, money, and trips to the hospital radiology department. We could now perform these tests at the patient's home. Convenient. The staple of any concierge practice. Our patients loved convenient.

While Evan drove, Divya rode shotgun. I sat in the back with my laptop hooked up to the plasma screen that folded down from the ceiling. It wasn't the forty-two-inch one that Evan had originally wanted but rather a more manageable thirty-two inches.

"Check this out," Evan said. "I can put the GPS map up on the screen back there."

Immediately the image of my laptop screen disappeared, replaced by the navigation window..

"Pretty cool," I said. "Now can I have my laptop back?"

"Don't you want to see where we're going?"

"I can look out the window for that. Right now I have to get these files up to date."

Evan tapped the dashboard touchscreen and the image on the plasma screen reverted to my laptop.

"I hesitate to say this," Divya said, "but I'm really impressed with the van. I had my doubts, but I must admit it has definitely made our job easier."

"Evan R. Lawson at your service. That's my job. To make your life easier."

"And when you're not as annoying as a green fly, you do fairly well in that regard."

Evan picked up his cell phone from where it lay in a central console tray and extended it toward Divya. "Would you say that again?"

"Not likely. In fact if I get a chance to erase all the other stuff you've recorded, I will."

"Too late. I've uploaded it to my cloud."

"The cloud that floats around in your brain?"

"Funny," Evan said.

It was. I laughed. Evan glared at me in the rearview mirror.

"Don't encourage her," he said.

"I need no encouragement," Divya said.

Evan R. Lawson is right.

"Put that down."

He did.

"Regardless," Evan said, "I'm glad you're mature enough to say I'm right when I'm right."

"Whether the van was useful or not was never a question," I said. "The problem was being able to afford it. And to your credit, you did work that out."

Evan's cell phone rang. He glanced at the screen as he picked it up.

"Speaking of paying for it." He punched the speakerphone button. "Hi, Rachel."

"Sorry to bother you but I wondered if either Hank or Divya could come by and take a look at one of my workers."

Rachel Fleming and her father owned Fleming's Custom Shop, the birthplace of the HankMed van. Evan's stroke of genius was to negotiate a deal where we got the use of the van for two years and then owned it in exchange for providing health care to their employees. We performed their employment physicals and took care of injuries and illnesses that occurred at the shop.

"What happened?" I asked.

"Oh, hi, Hank," Rachel said. "One of the guys grabbed a hot muffler. Burned his hand pretty badly. I told him to put some ice on it. I hope that was the right thing to do?"

"That's exactly the right thing to do. We're on our way."

Evan ended the call.

"I guess you can program your GPS to actually take us somewhere," I said. "Like Fleming's Custom Shop in Westhampton."

"But I know where that is," Evan said.

"I just hoped fiddling with it would keep you occupied while I finish my notes."

Evan punched in the address and a blue line appeared on the dashboard map display. "Got it," he said.

"That was quick," I said.

"Evan R. Lawson is a master programmer."

I shook my head. "Okay, master programmer, follow the little blue line and let Divya and me get some work done."

"Divya's not working."

Divya pulled her schedule book from her purse. "Now I am."

It took only fifteen minutes to reach Fleming's. Evan swung into the lot and parked between two freshly waxed vans, one black with huge windows on each side, the other a bright metallic blue with a California surf scene on the side.

Rachel came out the front door and walked toward us. She gave Evan a hug.

My brother the charmer.

"These new?" I asked, indicating the vans.

"Hot off the press. Customers are coming to pick them up around noon."

"I like the blue one," Evan said.

"A guy is buying it for his son. He's nineteen and

moving to LA for school. Big into surfing, so this is what we came up with for him. The kid has no idea. I'm sure he'll freak."

"Who wouldn't?" Evan said.

Well, I wouldn't for one, I thought. But then I'm not a West Coast surfer dude.

"Come on," Rachel said.

We followed her inside. She led us down a hallway to the break room, where we found Ralph Beacon sitting at a wooden table with his forearm resting palm up on the surface. He cupped a baggie filled with ice in his hand.

I sat down across from him. "How did this happen?"

"A guy we did a job for a couple of weeks ago came in saying his muffler was making some odd noises. He was in a hurry, so I got right on it. But"—he shrugged—"I got a little ahead of myself and didn't think that the muffler might be hot."

I lifted the ice bag. Several large blisters surrounded by erythematous tissue covered his palm. So did a greasy coating.

"What's this?"

"Butter. My mother always said to put butter on a burn."

"That's not exactly the best thing," I said. "It tends to hold the heat in and make the injury worse. The ice is good, but the butter not so much."

Divya opened the medical bag and pulled out a pack of sterilized instruments and gauze. She handed me a bottle of Betadine solution. I soaked a square of gauze with it and grasped his wrist firmly.

"This is going to be a little uncomfortable, but I have to clean it and get all this butter off."

"Go ahead. Couldn't be any worse than grabbing that muffler."

I gently washed his hand, removing the butter and cleaning the damaged skin as best I could. Then we walked to the sink, where Divya rinsed his hand with a bottle of sterilized water. I patted it dry with a wad of sterile gauze and we returned to the table.

I pulled on a pair of surgical gloves while Divya opened up the instrument kit. I removed the sterile tweezers and scissors inside.

"The burn has probably damaged the skin nerves in the area, so this shouldn't hurt much. If any. I just need to empty out these blisters."

It took only a couple of minutes to open them and drain the yellowish fluid that had collected inside. I then smeared the area with Silvadene cream, layered on a nonadherent Telfa pad, and stuffed the palm of his hand with a wad of sterile gauze. Finally, I wrapped his entire hand with gauze strips and taped it. It looked as if he was wearing a white cotton boxing glove.

"Not exactly a Band-Aid, is it?" Ralph said.

"It might look like overkill, but this is how an injured hand needs to be dressed. It's called the position of function. Sort of a half fist. Makes the healing go better, with less chance of complications." I smiled. "Of course, you're going to have to keep this clean and dry.

I'll give you a prescription for some pain medications and antibiotics. I'll also arrange for you to see a hand surgeon tomorrow."

"Is that necessary?"

"You don't want to mess with this. If it heals well you'll never have trouble with it. But if it gets infected, it can blossom into a really nasty third-degree injury and that changes the whole ball game. Surgery, skin grafting, loss of use of your hand, things like that."

He smiled. "You don't sugarcoat it, do you, Doc?"

"Sometimes. But not with something like this."

He glanced up at Rachel and then back to me. "What about work? I'll still be able to work, won't I?"

"Only if you can do something that doesn't require your hand. And something that will keep it clean and dry."

"I think a few days off might be best," Rachel said.

Ralph shrugged. "I have some vacation days built up. I can use them."

"You also have sick days," Rachel said. "Let's use those so you'll get paid."

"How can I turn that down?" Ralph stood. He looked at his bandaged hand and then at me. "Thanks, Doc."

Ralph left the break room.

"How's the health fair going?" Rachel asked.

"Great," Evan said. "We have all the sponsors lined up and all but two of the booths sold. Tell your dad thanks for ponying up for one of them."

"You guys are going to have a booth there?" I asked.

"We'll be there promoting our sports nut line."

"Sports nut line?"

Rachel laughed. "It was actually my idea but Dad jumped on it as soon as I told him. It's really called our Sports Enthusiast Edition. We configure vans and SUVs for various sports. We have one for skiers, one for surfers, scuba divers, and even soccer moms."

"What exactly do you do?" I asked.

"You saw the surfer one outside. And we just finished one for a scuba diving group. We created a custom top rack to hold an inflatable boat and racks in the back compartment for storing the tanks and other equipment. We even mounted an air compressor for refilling the tanks."

"Clever."

"Thank you. We can change out the roof racks so that the buyer can carry everything from canoes to skis. And we can configure the rear storage area to accommodate almost anything. Dozens of baseball bats and balls, surfboards, cross-country skis, you name it."

"Sounds like it's been successful."

Rachel nodded. "Amazingly so. We've been doing it for a year and at last count we'd sold twenty-three units."

"Maybe you'll sell some more at the health fair," Evan said.

"That's the hope."

Rachel led us back into the parking lot, where Divya and I climbed into the HankMed van. Evan stood at the open driver's-side door.

"We still on for lunch later this week?" Rachel asked.

"Absolutely. Any day better than another for you?"

"My dance card is fairly open."

Evan climbed into the van.

"Call me later and we'll decide," Rachel said.

"Cool."

Rachel pushed the door shut, turned, and headed back inside.

"Hmmm," I said as Evan pulled out of the lot and merged with traffic.

"What?" he asked.

"Nothing."

"We're just friends."

"That's what I thought."

"No, really."

Chapter 3

"He's in his room," Rosemary Moxley said. "Where he always is."

Rosemary had been a HankMed patient for at least a year. She had called, saying that her son, Kevin, was acting odd. Odd how? Moody, isolated, angry. Sounded like a typical teenager to me, but the worry in her voice was real. Rosemary was not the worrying type, so if she had concerns about her son so did I.

After leaving Fleming's Custom Shop, we had swung by Shadow Pond and dropped Evan off so he could head to his sponsor appointments. We then picked up coffee at Jill's favorite spot and detoured by the high school to take it to her. "Grateful" doesn't do her reaction justice. Rosemary's call came while we were talking with Jill.

We now sat at a rectangular wooden table in Rosemary's breakfast nook, a spacious and open area adjacent to the kitchen. Through the windows I saw a tree-shaded pool, a half dozen leaves floating on its surface. Slanted rays of morning sunlight dappled the surrounding deck.

"What exactly has been going on?" I asked.

She dabbed her tear-reddened eyes with a napkin that she then wadded in her hand. "It all started last year. I know you remember when my husband died."

I did. Rosemary took it hard. Depression mixed with anxiety and the sleep deprivation that invariably accompanies that combination. It had been rocky, but she'd weathered it with the help of the right medication and a good psychiatrist.

"Of course."

"Kev never really recovered from losing him. I almost didn't either." She offered a weak smile and then sniffed back tears. "His schoolwork suffered. He quit baseball and basketball. Started using marijuana."

She took a deep breath and stared beyond me toward the wall for a minute. I waited, giving her time to get the story out at her own pace.

"He became withdrawn," Rosemary continued. "Moody and sullen. Didn't often go out with his friends. Still doesn't. And that used to be a constant problem. Really the only thing we argued over. He wanted to be with his friends all the time, but we wouldn't allow him to be out every night like he wanted. Now he stays locked up in his room. He rarely eats and has lost . . . I don't know . . . I'd guess twenty pounds. He certainly didn't need to." She fell silent and stared at her hands, now folded on the table before her.

"What happened today that prompted you to call us?" Divya asked.

"He's different."

"How?" I asked.

"He's hyped up. Jittery. He seems confused and doesn't make much sense when he talks."

"Confused?" Divya asked. "In what way?"

"I made breakfast this morning. He didn't really eat any. Maybe a few bites. The whole time he talked about all sorts of stuff. Jumping from one topic to another. Like a runaway train. Kept tapping on the table and bouncing his leg." She looked at me. "It's drugs, isn't it?"

I nodded. "Could be. How old is Kevin now?"

"Sixteen."

"Can I go talk with him?"

"Please." She stood.

"I mean alone."

She hesitated.

"It might be best. He's more likely to tell me the truth."

She collapsed into her chair again. "I suppose that's true. Lord knows he won't talk to me." She nodded toward a hall across the dining room from where we sat. "His room is the last door on the right."

I grabbed my medical bag and walked that way. The hallway was lined with family photos. Some were of Rosemary and her late husband. Others were older. Black and white and grainy. Probably the grandparents. But most were of Kevin. As a baby, in a crib, butt bare, head up with a wide toothless grin. As a very young boy in a cowboy outfit, cap pistol aimed at the photographer, black hat pulled low over his eyes, a snarl on his face. Trying to look like an outlaw, no doubt. Others were school and sports photos, several of baseball and basketball teams.

I rapped on the door. "Kevin?" No response. I rapped harder. "Kevin?" I called, a little louder this time. Still no answer. I pushed the door open.

Kevin sat at a desk, his back to me, earbuds jammed in his ears, a music video on his laptop, head bobbing, hands playing air drums.

"Kevin?"

Still no response.

I walked over and tapped his shoulder. He jumped and whirled around, tugging the buds from his ears.

"Who are you?"

His face was sweat-slicked, pupils dilated. His gaze bounced around the room.

"You don't remember me?" I asked.

He stared blankly.

"I'm Dr. Lawson. Your mother's doctor."

"Oh. Yeah?" His knee bounced to an internal rhythm now.

"She wanted me to talk with you."

"About what?"

"May I?" I motioned toward the bed next to his desk.

"Sure."

I sat.

He wiped his palms on his jeans and eyed me suspiciously.

"How are you doing?" I asked.

"Fine. What's this about? I mean, I have things to do so I don't have much time."

"What things?"

That seemed to confuse him.

"You know. Things." He looked around the room. "Lots of things."

"Kevin," I said. His gaze snapped back to me. "What did you take?"

"Nothing, dude. Why would you ask that?" Another swipe of his palms on his jeans, this time leaving behind moist streaks.

"Is it okay if I examine you?"

"What do you mean?"

"Just listen to your heart and lungs. That sort of thing."

"Why?"

"To humor your mom. She's worried. If I find you're okay I can reassure her."

The little white lies we tell to get patients to do the right thing. The truth was that I was as worried as she was. Maybe more so, if that was possible. Just looking at Kevin told me he was on speed. Or meth or some other upper. Didn't take a genius to see that.

"Only take a minute," I continued.

"Okay, I guess."

I checked his blood pressure. Elevated at one-eighty over one hundred. Heart rate one-ten. I then lifted his shirt and placed my stethoscope on his chest. I could feel his heart through my fingers as much as I could hear it. Hard and rapid. Almost leaping against his chest. I moved to his back. "A couple of deep breaths." He did. Clear. I folded my stethoscope and dropped it into my bag.

"I'm okay. Right?"

I smiled. "I need to check a couple more things. Hold your hands out flat. Palms down."

"Why?"

"Kevin, this'll only take a minute. Let's just get it over with. Okay?"

He extended his hands toward me. His fingers trembled. I then used my rubber reflex hammer to test his elbow and knee reflexes. Both exaggerated. I then aimed a penlight at his eyes. His pupils were widely dilated and only partially reacted to the light.

"I'd like to draw some blood."

"No."

"Why not?"

"What for?"

I took a deep breath and let it out slowly. "Look, Kevin. I know you're using something." He started to say something, but I stopped him with a raised hand. "It's got you all hyped up. Whatever it is, it's dangerous. Potentially deadly."

"No, it's not."

"What is it?"

"Nothing."

"Kevin?"

"It's nothing."

"Show me."

He hesitated, then stood and walked to his dresser. He removed a baggie from deep toward the back of the bottom drawer and handed it to me. Inside were three small pink pills.

"What are these?"

"They're called Strawberry Quick. They're feel-good pills. They make you feel happy."

"You don't look happy to me. You look frazzled. Worn-out."

He sat down again, his leg resuming its dance. "I'm fine."

"Really?" I saw a camera on his desk. "Let me see that."

He handed the digital camera to me. I examined it, quickly locating the ON/OFF button and the shutter release.

"Look at me," I said. He did and I snapped his picture, the flash causing him to recoil slightly. I handed him the camera. "Upload this to your computer."

He did and then opened the picture. I walked over and grabbed the photo of him that sat on his dresser. Looked like it had been taken maybe a year ago. He was smiling, a baseball cap slightly tilted on his head. I returned to where he sat and held it next to the laptop screen.

"What do you see?"

"Me."

"And?"

He studied them for a minute.

"See how handsome you were? When was this picture taken?"

"Last year."

"See the difference?"

It was stark. A year ago Kevin looked healthy, with full cheeks and bright eyes. Now his cheeks were sunken, dark bags hung beneath his eyes, and his dilated pupils gave him a cornered-animal look.

"Let me show you something else."

I opened up his Web browser and typed *methamphetamine* into the search window. A list of links popped up. I selected the one titled "Meth User Photos." An array of thumbnails appeared. I enlarged one of a young man about Kevin's age and moved it until that photo and the one I had just taken were side by side.

"See this?" I indicated the framed photo. "This is where you were a year ago." I then pointed to the computer screen and the picture I had just taken of him. "This is where you are now. And this—" I now pointed out the meth user's photo. "This is where you're headed."

He stared at the user's photo. The young man had deeply sunken cheeks, recessed, dark eyes, and sores and scabs over his face. His teeth were yellowed and deformed.

Kevin's eyes widened further.

"This stuff will kill you." I held up the baggie. "It's methamphetamine."

His knee bounced higher, faster, but his gaze dropped and held the floor.

"You know what that is?"

He shrugged. "They told me it was harmless."

"It's packaged to look that way. Why do you think it's pretty and pink and called by such a harmless name? How could something called Strawberry Quick be harmful? It sounds so fresh and clean. Like a new Kool-Aid flavor." I wiggled the bag. "It's all marketing, Kevin. Just to get you hooked. Then they'll own you."

He gave me a brief glance and then dropped his gaze back toward the floor.

"Let me ask you this." His gaze rose again. "Is this how you saw your life back then?" I pointed to his year-old picture. "When you were playing sports and had friends? When you actually laughed?"

Tears collected in his eyes. "No." He sniffed and swiped the back of one hand over his nose.

"Don't you think it's time to turn back the clock?"

"Maybe." The knee started again. "I don't know."

"Who sold this to you?"

"I don't want to get anybody in trouble."

"Whoever sells this stuff is not your friend."

"I know."

"Then who did you get these from?" I held up the bag.

"I don't know."

I sighed and then stood.

"What are you going to do?"

"Talk with your mom."

He reached for the baggie, but I moved it out of reach.

"Those are mine," he said.

"Not anymore." I walked to the door and turned back. "Sorry, but I can't stand by and let you kill yourself." I waved the bag. "And these will do exactly that." I nodded toward his computer. "Study those pictures. Really look at them. That could be you."

Chapter 4

"I've been hearing good things about the health fair," George Shanahan said. "It seems like everybody I know is going."

George Shanahan was everything Evan admired. Wealthy, cool, well dressed, and president of Hamptons Savings and Loan. He brokered deals for some of the most expensive property in the Hamptons and therefore the world. He helped some of the world's wealthiest families manage their real estate investments and their sizable portfolios. He rubbed elbows with presidents and heads of states, never mind senators and congressmen and Fortune 500 CEOs.

Shanahan sat behind his expansive desk with his perfectly manicured hands folded before him. He wore an expensive gray suit that highlighted the slight graying at his temples. His pale blue eyes were alive and his smile almost electric.

"It's going to be big," Evan said. "There'll be events for kids of all ages. Even a charity walk on Sunday."

"Count us in for that. My wife, Betsy, is already psyched up for it. She's been training."

"We already have over two hundred walkers signed up."

"That many?"

"It'll be bigger. I'd bet even more people will sign up at the event."

Shanahan nodded. "What about your fund-raising? Has that been going well, too?"

"It's so cool. We've passed our goal. Thanks to people like you."

Evan considered George Shanahan a real coup. Not that Shanahan didn't give generously and often to charity, but getting an appointment with him was no easy task. His daily schedule seemed always filled with buyers, sellers, big-dollar investors, and other bankers. The kind of people who wore suits to work. Expensive suits. Custom-tailored suits. Evan tried for weeks to get a sit-down but had no luck. He even showed up in a suit one day. Not all that expensive a suit, but a suit nonetheless. Nothing. No way past the gatekeeper—Claire, Shanahan's stern, all-business, middle-aged secretary.

Until he softened her up with the old Evan R. Lawson charm, that is. And a box of chocolates. And flowers. Finally, she gave in. Said she'd never seen anyone try so hard. She even smiled as she looked at him over the half-glasses she wore roped around her neck. That was last week. And once Evan had made it inside the inner sanctum, Shanahan didn't hesitate to offer a very generous donation.

Shanahan shrugged. "Hamptons Savings and Loan has been part of this community for a long time. Since my father started the business. I feel a personal obligation to support worthy causes, and I can't think of one better than a health and fitness fair that supports our hospital, school, and Jill Casey's community clinic. I've been hearing very good things about it."

"She is ferocious about it," Evan said. "It's her baby and she takes it very seriously."

Shanahan pulled open a drawer and removed a check. He gave it a wrist snap and then handed it to Evan. "I know it's a little more than I had promised. I hope you don't mind." He smiled.

Evan looked at the amount. "Mind? Dude, this is so generous. Thanks."

"As I said, this is my community, too."

The intercom on his phone buzzed and he punched a button.

"Mr. Shanahan, your appointment is here."

"Thanks, Claire." He stood and walked Evan to the door. "I ran into Nathan Zimmer the other day. Hank-Med came up."

"Oh?"

"He said he's very impressed with you and Hank. Divya, too, of course."

"I'm impressed with him, too," Evan said.

"He said you were all coming to his big party."

"Yes, we are."

His hand rested on the door handle, but he hesitated. "Nathan's parties are always over the top."

"I know. That's why we're having trouble deciding what to wear."

Shanahan laughed. "Join the crowd. My wife can't either. And until she does, I can't."

"I'm thinking maybe a spy would be cool. What do you think?"

Shanahan studied him for a minute. "Maybe the town crier. Or a newspaper publisher." He snapped his fingers. "I've got it. A bookkeeper. You'd make a great bookkeeper."

Why did everyone keep saying that?

Two police officers arrived at the Moxley home ten minutes after Rosemary called. And she called as soon as I showed her the baggie of pink pills.

Sergeant Willard McCutcheon appeared to be a grizzled veteran. Thick-chested, massive forearms hanging from his uniform sleeves, crew-cut pewter hair—he looked like a Marine Corps drill instructor. Ex-military for sure. He oozed no-nonsense. His partner, Officer Tommy Griffin, was young. In fact, he looked too young to be a police officer. More like one of Kevin's classmates. Dirty blond hair, clear blue eyes, and a square jaw that I wasn't sure had ever needed shaving.

The two stood side by side, leaning against the kitchen counter. McCutcheon hooked his thumbs over his belt as he looked down at Kevin. The boy shrank in his chair under his gaze. Rosemary sat next to her son, stern-faced, arms crossed over her chest.

"Answer their questions," Rosemary said.

So far, Kevin had only sulked, head down, refusing, except for an occasional glance, to even look at the officers.

"Mom, I'll get in trouble," Kevin mumbled into his own chest.

"You're already in trouble, son," McCutcheon said.

Kevin fidgeted and finally looked up. "I didn't do anything."

"The mere possession of methamphetamine is a felony. You know what that means?"

Kevin stared at him, his expression flat.

"It means we could arrest you, take you downtown, stand you up before the judge, and you'd end up in juvenile detention until you're eighteen. Is that what you want?"

I was standing behind Rosemary and sensed her body stiffen at McCutcheon's words. I gently touched her shoulder.

Kevin mumbled something and then swallowed hard. Or tried to. I could tell his mouth was cotton-dry.

"I didn't get that," McCutcheon said. "Is that what you want us to do? Haul you in?"

"No," Kevin said.

"Then tell us what we need to know."

Kevin's gaze returned to his lap.

I moved to Kevin's side and squatted down next to him, my eyes now level with his. He looked at me.

"Listen to me," I said.

His knee began bouncing again.

"I know you think you're protecting your friends. I know you're scared. But I also know your mother. She raised you to do the right thing. And from what I hear, until the last year or so you were doing exactly that."

He shrugged.

"Every young man has to grow up and become a man. I did. Sergeant McCutcheon did. Your dad did." He looked up at me. "What do you think he'd say if he was here?"

"But he isn't."

"No, he's not. And that means you have more responsibility. Your mother is counting on you."

Rosemary removed a napkin from the holder that sat in the middle of the table. She dabbed her eyes.

"You love her, don't you?"

"Of course," he mumbled.

"Then show her. What do you think she would do without you? Your dad isn't here. And if you're locked up she'll be alone. Is that what you want?"

"No."

"Then do what you know is right."

He sighed and then mumbled something, but I couldn't understand him.

"What?"

He looked up at me and then toward McCutcheon. "I don't know them. They're not students."

"How many?" McCutcheon asked.

"Two. A dude and his girlfriend."

Officer Griffin pulled out a notepad and began scribbling in it.

"You know their names?" McCutcheon asked.

"No." Kevin shook his head. "Pete and Erin is all I know."

"What do they look like?"

"Pete is tall and thin. Maybe your height but much smaller. He has long hair. Sometimes it's in a ponytail about this long." He held up his hands, palms about a foot apart.

"How old?"

"I don't know."

"Facial hair?"

Kevin shook his head.

"The girl?" McCutcheon said. "I think you said Erin was her name."

"She's short. Wears jeans and oversized T-shirts. Or she did the couple of times I've seen her. She has long hair, too. Really long. Down to her waist."

"Color?"

"Dark brown. Stringy. Looks like she doesn't wash it much."

"They hang around the school?"

"I guess."

"What do you mean, 'guess'?"

"I've never seen them there, but I know some people who have."

"Where did you meet them?" McCutcheon asked.

"In a parking lot. Down near the beach."

"Which lot?"

"Down behind that restaurant. The one with the big blue fish sign out front."

McCutcheon spun a chair around and sat across from Kevin. He leaned one forearm on the chair's back. It was as thick as my leg.

"Here's the deal, Kevin. We aren't going to arrest you or charge you with anything if you'll do a couple of things for me."

"What?"

"If you see them again, call me."

"Okay."

"And give us the names of the other people you know who have dealt with them."

"I can't do that."

"Why?" McCutcheon asked.

"Mom?" Kevin said, giving his mother a plaintive look.

"Do what they ask, Kev. You have to."

"But I'll be a snitch. No one will talk to me."

"They'll never know," McCutcheon said. "We won't use your name."

Kevin hesitated and then nodded. "Okay."

After Kevin came clean, Divya and I walked out with McCutcheon and Griffin.

"Have you guys seen much of this?" I asked. "This new kid-friendly meth?"

McCutcheon had the passenger door to their cruiser open. He propped one arm on the doorframe and looked at me. "A couple." He looked across the roof to where Griffin was pulling open the driver's-side door.

"When was the last one?" I asked.

"What—three weeks ago? Some kid got all squirrelly. Ended up in the ER. Wouldn't say a word about where he got it. Labs showed amphetamines."

"Hadn't that kid taken some ecstasy, too?" Griffin said.

"That's right," McCutcheon said, shaking his head. "The things kids will do nowadays."

"The amphetamine the kid took, was it this same Strawberry Quick stuff?" I asked.

"Don't know," McCutcheon said. "He didn't have any on him and, as I said, he refused to answer our questions."

I nodded. "I've read a little about this in the medical journals. Seems to be a new way of packaging an old drug."

McCutcheon held up the plastic bag and looked at the two pink pills inside. "Pretty sinister. Making that garbage look like valentine candy."

"That's the marketing plan," I said. "Make it look innocent. Fun. Safe."

McCutcheon sighed. "We'll get this over to the lab and see what's in it."

"Could you give me a call when you know? I need to get the word out to the local ERs about what we're dealing with." I handed him my card.

"Will do. Hopefully this is just a couple of isolated deals. Hate to think we were going to have another drug epidemic like we had fifteen years ago when cocaine was everywhere." He glanced over at Griffin. "Before your time."

"Thanks for coming out," I said. I glanced back toward the house. "My gut tells me Kevin is a good kid. Just got himself mixed up in something."

"Isn't that the way it usually is?" McCutcheon said. "Peer pressure is a dangerous thing."

Amen to that.

McCutcheon handed me his card. "If you see or hear about any other cases, give me a call."

"Will do."

Divya and I watched as they drove away.

"Why would anyone make something like that?" Divya asked. "Target kids that way?"

"Money trumps all."

After leaving Shanahan's office, Evan walked the two blocks down Main Street to Marcy's Bodyworks, a popular yoga and Pilates studio. There were several in the Hamptons, but Marcy's was at the top of the food chain. Where all the beautiful people worked out. Even a few Hollywood celebrities and high-end New York fashion models. Evan could have sworn the last time he was there he saw one of the Victoria's Secret models. Marcy was considering taking a booth at the health fair but hadn't quite decided. She'd said she would have an answer for him today.

When Evan entered the studio he was greeted by a smile from Stephanie, the receptionist.

"Evan," she said. "How's it going?"

"Fine. I think I'm a little early for my appointment with Marcy."

"A little. She's just finishing up a class and should be out in a minute. Can I get you something to drink?"

"Maybe one of those cool lemon waters you guys have?" Evan said.

"I think I have some right here."

She spun in her chair and pulled open the small refrigerator she kept behind the reception desk. Evan heard glass rattling and then Stephanie straightened and extended a bottle toward him.

"Here you go."

Evan twisted off the cap and took a swig. "I love this stuff."

"Me, too. I must drink ten a day."

The front door opened and two young brunette women came in. They looked like sisters. Or clones. Same height and weight. Each wore white shorts and a silk shirt, one dark green, the other lemon yellow. Each had a tan canvas sports bag dangling from one shoulder.

"Hey, Stephanie," the green-shirted one said.

The lemon yellow looked at Evan and smiled.

"You guys are early today," Stephanie said.

"Yeah. We're going into the city later so we decided to come to Marcy's earlier class."

"Have fun."

"We will."

They headed toward the dressing area. Just as they pushed through the door, lemon yellow glanced back at Evan and smiled again.

"Who was that?" Evan asked.

"Zoe and Amy. Two of our regulars."

"Are they sisters?"

"Everyone asks that. No, but they look like it, don't they?"

"Sure do. Which one was wearing yellow?"

Stephanie laughed. "The one that kept looking at you?"

Evan felt his face redden. He nodded. "Yeah."

"That's Amy. And she's unattached." Stephanie leaned back in her chair, crossing her arms. "In case you're wondering."

"Who wouldn't? She's beautiful."

"One of the advantages of being a member. You should join. It would do you good." She laughed again. "And not just in the fitness department."

"Maybe I will. As long as Marcy doesn't try to kill me with her workouts."

"She usually does," Stephanie said.

"She usually does what?"

Evan turned to see Marcy. She was wearing tight capri pants and a form-fitting sleeveless tank top, both black. A white towel hung over one shoulder. Her skin appeared flushed and glistened with sweat from her workout. Her short black hair was damp, with a few ringlets plastered to the side of her head.

"You usually work us too hard," Stephanie said. She handed Marcy a bottle of lemon water.

"That's what I'm here for. And when I finish hammering my clients I go out and pull the wings off small bugs." She looked at Evan. "When are you and Hank going to join one of our classes?"

"We were just talking about that," Evan said. "I can, but for Hank the problem is finding the time."

"You've got to make the time. It's important." She jerked her head toward the hallway. "Come on. Let's head down to my office."

Her office was small and spartan. A simple office furniture megastore desk and three chairs, phone, and laptop computer. Bookshelves filled with fitness books and manuals covered one wall. A single large window, horizontal blinds cranked open, looked out onto Main Street. Marcy sat down behind her desk. She wiped her face with the towel, twisted the top off the water, and downed several healthy gulps. Evan took one of the two chairs that faced her.

Evan got right to it. "So what do you think? We're down to the last booth."

Marcy nodded. "We're in."

"That's great. I was hoping you would be."

"Stephanie and I will be there most of the time. And a couple of the other instructors will be there part time."

"You're going to love your booth. It's just down from where the HankMed booth will be. Close to the entrance so everybody will have to walk by it to get anywhere."

Marcy pulled open her desk drawer and lifted out a checkbook. One of those large ledger types. She flipped it open and began writing. "A thousand for the week-end, right?"

"That's right."

"I'm sure we're going to more than make it up by signing up new clients and selling our logo clothing. If not, it's for a good cause."

She handed the check to Evan. He looked at it, folded it, and slipped it into his shirt pocket.

"Thanks," he said. "I'll work on Hank and see if I can get him to join."

"What about you? You could sign up even if Hank can't."

"Of course. Evan R. Lawson was built for Pilates."

Marcy raised an eyebrow. "I'll tell Stephanie to put you in one of my classes and we'll see."

Chapter 5

Felicia Hecht was fifty-two, widowed, and lived in a modest home near the water in Sag Harbor. She led us into her living room, where she settled onto an intricately patterned green love seat, Divya and I on the matching sofa across a glass-topped coffee table from her. The room was pastel green. The mantel over the stone fireplace held several framed photos. One of her and I presumed the late Mr. Hecht, another of a young woman who could only be her daughter, standing with a man behind two young children. Nice-looking family.

She offered us coffee or something to drink, but we declined.

"I told Dr. Lawson about your symptoms," Divya said. "The headaches and nausea."

Felicia looked at me. "They're very odd."

"Tell me about them."

"The headaches start around here," she said, indicating her right temple. "And then the whole right side of my head hurts. My face sometimes."

"How long do they usually last?"

"Mostly a half hour or so, but sometimes most of the day. I just never know. When it comes on I always pray it will go away quickly. Sometimes they even keep me up at night."

"How long has this been going on?"

She offered a sheepish grin. "A few months."

"And you haven't talked to anyone about it yet?" Divya asked.

"It was so odd I wasn't even sure who to see. I thought maybe it was all in my head. Due to stress or something like that." She sighed. "But the other day I told Ellie Wentworth about them, and she said I should call you. That you're the best doctor in the world and that if anyone can figure it out, you can. So here you are."

Ellie Wentworth was one of my favorite patients. Astoundingly wealthy, she lived in an East Hampton mansion and was famous for her hugely successful theme parties. She was also one of the most down-to-earth people I'd ever known, proving that rich people can be real people.

"That's nice of her to say," I said, feeling a bit uncomfortable. Glowing praise had always done that to me.

"I trust her, so that's why I called."

"We're glad you did," I said. "Is there anything you can relate these headaches to? Something you do or eat or anything that might make this more likely to happen?"

"Maybe red wine. Maybe chocolate." She looked at me, her head cocked slightly. "But if you tell me I can't have chocolate, I'll find another doctor." She laughed.

"Hopefully that's not part of it. But—" I shrugged, my hands open. "Sometimes chocolate can make migraine-type headaches worse."

"Is that what I have?"

"Maybe. You mentioned stress. Have you been stressed lately?"

"No more than usual." She glanced at Divya. "But my friends tell me I worry too much." She smiled. "I have to admit that I do."

"Can you relate the headaches to stress?" Divya asked.

"Maybe. But to be honest I can't tell which comes first. The worry or the pain. I mean, the pain makes me worry, but I'm not sure me being stressed really causes the pain. Does that make sense?"

I nodded. "Perfectly."

"So what is it?"

"I have a couple of ideas, but let me examine you and get some tests done first."

Divya checked her blood pressure and pulse, saying they were normal except her pulse was slightly elevated at ninety-five. Her EKG showed the same but was otherwise normal.

"I'm nervous," Felicia said.

"That would explain it," I said as I stood, walked

around the coffee table, and sat down next to her. "Just relax. I don't bite."

Her lungs were clear and her cardiac exam normal, as were her carotid pulsations. I did a brief neurologic exam, which was also normal. I then palpated along the side of her head and temple.

"Is any of this uncomfortable?" I asked, my fingers pressing into the soft area beneath her jaw.

"No. And when it's hurting I'll press there, too, but it doesn't seem to make any difference. It seems deeper than that."

Divya was taking notes, so I said to her, "I don't feel any masses or nodes. Her parotid gland is normal and nontender and there're no areas of tenderness to suggest temporal arteritis or TMJ."

"What are those?"

"Things you don't have." I smiled.

"So what is it?"

"Most likely what we call a mixed headache. That's one with multiple causes. In your situation they are probably due to stress, perhaps with a migraine component."

"Migraines? I had a friend with those. They'd put her in bed for days sometimes."

I nodded. "They can. But yours seem milder. At least so far."

"What do I do?"

"We'll draw some blood for a few tests and I'll give you a couple of prescriptions. One for pain, and a mild tranquilizer for when you feel stressed."

Divya drew the blood while I wrote out the pre-scriptions.

"Try these. They should help." I handed them to her. "I'll call as soon as we get the labs back."

As Divya and I worked our way south from Sag Harbor toward Shadow Pond to hook up with Evan for lunch, Evan called. He was at a sandwich shop waiting for his order to be prepared. He suggested that rather than meeting at home we meet at the high school. He needed to talk with Jill.

"Actually that works out better," I said. "We should take a look at our booth and I've got a couple of things to talk about with Jill, too."

"I'll meet you at the HankMed booth. Do you know where it is?"

"Jill said it was the first one on the left when you come through the entry gate. Should be easy to find."

It was. But when we arrived there was no Evan and I didn't see Jill anywhere. I gave her a call, but she couldn't talk, saying she was in the middle of something but would be over in a few minutes. As I hung up, Evan arrived.

"Where's Jill?" Evan asked.

"Busy. She'll be here in a minute."

Evan placed a bag on the table. "Lunch is served." He began pulling plastic containers out and setting them on one of the two exam tables that were in the booth.

"Where did these come from?" Evan asked.

I stared at him. "What do you mean? You bought them. Just a few minutes ago."

"I didn't mean the sandwiches; I meant the exam tables. And that desk."

A desk and a single chair sat toward the back of the canvas-covered booth and an exam table along each wall. I also noticed there were bright orange electrical cords stretching across the grass near the back of the booth and disappearing under the canvas in each direction. Two multi-plug outlets nestled among the electrical cables. Jill's work, I was sure.

Divya popped open one of the plastic containers and lifted out half a sandwich. She took a bite.

"These are excellent," she said. "Where did you get them?"

"You know that little sandwich shop over in East Hampton? The one on the corner?"

"Yes, but I've never been in there."

"I go there all the time," Evan said. "They also make great soups and pastries."

I bit into a sandwich. It was good. And big. Ham and Swiss with crisp lettuce and fresh tomatoes stuffed between two slices of homemade wheat bread, it was a meal and then some.

Jill showed up.

"Sorry I'm late. I had a meeting with the EMS director. He'll have a couple of his crews here throughout the weekend and we needed to go over some things."

I handed her a sandwich and she took a bite.

"Thanks. I haven't had anything since coffee early this morning."

"I take it this is all your doing?" I waved a hand toward the desk and exam tables.

"These were stored in the hospital's basement, collecting dust. I figured you could use them. Better than renting."

"And cheaper," Evan said.

"It's so nice that our CFO is fiscally responsible," Divya said.

Evan pointed a pickle spear at her. "Just looking after the bottom line." He took a bite of the pickle. "I have some good news."

"Like what?" Jill asked.

"I rented the last booth. To Marcy Davidson." He removed two checks from his pocket and handed one to Jill.

"That's great. I was afraid half the booths would be empty."

"Not with Evan R. Lawson on the case."

"You're a case, all right," Divya said.

"But I keep you in business. Jill, too, apparently."

"You've been outstanding," Jill said. "You know that, don't you? I could never have pulled this off without you." She looked at me and then at Divya. "You two also."

"It's even better." Evan handed her the other check. "This is from George Shanahan over at Hamptons Savings and Loan."

Jill looked at it. "This is even more than he promised."

"He couldn't resist the old Evan R. Lawson charm."

Divya rolled her eyes. "Spare me. He probably gave you the extra to get you out of his office."

"Wish I could afford that," I said.

"Tease all you want," Evan said, "but this brings our total to fifty percent more than our goal."

Jill looked stunned. "You're kidding. That much?"

"I would never lie about money." Evan laid one hand on his chest as if reciting the Pledge of Allegiance.

"How on earth did you pull that off?"

"I guess I'm a salesman extraordinaire. You might even say a supersalesman."

"Silly me. I thought you were a superspy," Divya said.

"That, too." He picked up his cell phone.

Evan R. Lawson is a superspy.

Divya glared at him. "I swear I'm going to steal your phone and flush it."

Evan R. Lawson is right.

Divya shook her head. "Unbelievable."

Jill took a final bite of her sandwich and wadded up the paper around the little bit that was left. She stood. "I need to get back to work. What are you guys up to?"

"A couple of patients to see," I said.

"Dinner still on for tonight?" Jill asked while rummaging in her purse for her sunglasses.

"Around seven."

She looked at Evan. "This is becoming a habit with you. Are you going to cook every night?"

"It's my domestic side," he said.

"Too bad you don't have a domesticated side," Divya said.

Jill settled her sunglasses in place. "I'll bring some wine. What do you plan to cook?"

"I'm not sure yet. Just bring red."

My cell phone rang.

Chapter 6

The call was from Todd Hammersmith, Nathan Zimmer's assistant. One of the workers who had been prepping Nathan's mansion for the big Fourth of July costume party was having chest pain. Todd went back and forth between talking to me and to Nathan, whom I could hear in the background. Confusing to say the least, but that was Nathan. The story I finally got was that the man had been helping move a piano, had developed chest pain, and was now lying on the floor. Conscious? Yes. Breathing? Yes. Did they call 911? No. Why not? This led to more discussion between Todd and Nathan.

I finally interrupted and told Todd to call 911 and that I'd be right there.

"Right where?" Evan asked after I disconnected the call.

"Nathan Zimmer's place."

"Count me in," Evan said. "If you're going to see Nathan, I'm going."

Evan and his buddy Nathan. First-name basis. Slap on the back. Cigars and whiskey. I wondered if Nathan knew what good friends they were?

We climbed into the HankMed van, Divya driving, Evan riding shotgun, me in back. As she cranked the van to life, Divya said to Evan, "I thought you had appointments this afternoon."

"Dude, it's Nathan Zimmer."

"I'm not a dude," she said.

"Fooled me."

"Funny." Her brow wrinkled.

She accelerated through the gate and around the parking lot's perimeter. Pure NASCAR.

"Just being around Nathan makes me smarter," Evan said, clinging to the dash for balance.

"Perhaps if Nathan makes you so smart you should go to work for him."

"What would happen to HankMed then?"

"Nathan's loss would be our gain."

The tires squealed as Divya turned from the lot onto the street.

"Don't you have that backwards?" Evan asked. "Wouldn't it be Nathan's gain and your loss?"

"I think not."

"Go ahead. Make fun of me. But the smarter I am, the better HankMed does."

Divya raised an eyebrow. "And all this time I

thought it was because Hank and I did such stellar work."

"That, too. But it took smarts to arrange the Hank-Med van."

"True," I said. "You did good there."

"Being around people like Nathan Zimmer sparks such creative thinking."

"Sort of like a viral infection?" I asked. I should have stayed out of it, but I couldn't resist.

"Or the plague," Divya added.

"Or the seeds of great ideas," Evan replied.

"Seeds require fertile soil." Divya slung the van through a hard left turn, pressing Evan against the passenger door. I clutched the arms of my captain's chair.

"I have fertile soil," Evan said.

"You have rocks."

Their bickering continued during the twenty-minute drive. I tried to ignore them, but when they got to full boil there was no way. As Evan kept needling Divya, her foot got heavier. I held on as she weaved and swerved through traffic and took corners on what felt like two wheels. Somehow we survived Mr. Toad's Wild Ride and reached Nathan Zimmer's estate intact.

I grabbed the medical bag from the back and we climbed the broad stone steps to the mansion. Nathan's estate was nothing like Shadow Pond, which rivaled the best France's Loire Valley had to offer, looking like something King Louis would have built to escape Paris's summer heat. Nathan's version of a mansion was modern. Very modern. No French château here. All metal, glass, and acute angles. Still impressive, but in a very different way.

The front door stood open, so we walked in and followed the boot-printed paper pathway that stretched over the carpet to the great room. The room that was usually filled with very expensive furniture now stood mostly empty.

Its transformation into a colonial meetinghouse—or perhaps a presidential inauguration would be more like it—was well under way. A dozen flags and two massive crystal chandeliers hung from the thirty-foot ceiling. The stark white walls, glass, and chrome of the very modern home were now partially concealed behind flowing red, white, and blue striped drapes.

Nathan and Todd stood near one wall, looking over the shoulders of several workers kneeling around a man who was stretched out on the floor. The ever-present pulsing Bluetooth device hung from Nathan's left ear. Both he and Todd turned when we entered.

"Dr. Lawson, I'm glad you're here," Todd said.

"Did you call nine-one-one?" I asked.

"I thought it might be better to wait for you," Nathan said. "He thinks he might have just pulled something."

I approached the group. The workers stood and cleared a path for Divya and me. The man lay next to a massive and elaborate grand piano, which was up on a rolling platform as if ready to be moved. He looked to be in his fifties, with thinning hair now damp with sweat, as was his face. He wore jeans and a blue work shirt, the front and armpits darkened with perspiration. He held one hand clamped over his chest.

I knelt next to him, my fingers automatically reaching to check his carotid pulse. It was fast but steady. "What's the matter?"

The man was groaning and his words came out as gasps. "My chest. And my back." He rolled slightly back and forth. "I can't breathe."

This was no pulled muscle.

I listened to his heart and lungs. His heart rate was rapid, his lungs clear. Divya checked his blood pressures in both arms.

"I get two-twenty over one-twenty on the right side and one-forty over ninety on the left."

The concern I saw in her face told me that she was thinking the same thing I was.

"Do you have any medical problems?" I asked.

"High blood pressure. Had it for years."

"Do you take any medications?"

"A couple of pills for that, but I don't remember what they are. I ran out of them three or four days ago."

"So you haven't taken any meds for several days?"

He nodded. "My insurance company. They do this every month. They'll only send me thirty pills and then half the time they're a week late getting the new ones to me."

Not an uncommon problem. This is what happens when the money changers take over medicine. Everybody in a pigeonhole. Everybody in line. The dollar trumps science. God forbid that someone might waste a couple of three-cent pills. Better that they have too few than too many. Welcome to the new medicine.

I looked at Divya. "Get the crash kit and the portable X-ray from the van." I turned to Evan. "Help her bring the machine in."

One of the workers stepped forward. "Anything we can do?"

"If you could help them get the equipment that would be great."

He nodded. "Will do."

I returned to examining the man. "What's your name?"

"Jimmy Sutter."

"How old are you?"

"Fifty-two."

"What happened?"

"We were lifting the piano up on the platform there. So we can roll it out here. Just as we were settling it in place it hit me. Can you do something about this pain?"

"It's coming. Where does it hurt?"

"All across my chest." He ran his open palm from one side of his chest to the other. His breathing was still labored. "And in my back. Between my shoulder blades. It feels like something is ripping apart in there. You think I tore a muscle or something?"

"I'm going with the 'or something' right now."

"What is it, Doc?"

"Just relax. We should know in a few minutes."

Divya and the equipment arrived. While she started

an IV, I opened up the crash kit. I drew up some morphine, and as soon as the IV was in place, gave him five milligrams. I then gave him five milligrams of lisinopril and ten milligrams of metoprolol.

"That should help your pain and lower your blood pressure."

While Divya rechecked his blood pressure, I began setting up the X-ray.

"His blood pressure is coming down," Divya said. "I'm getting one-eighty over one hundred on the right and one-ten over sixty on the left."

I completed unfolding the X-ray machine and we gently moved Jimmy into position. I connected the machine to my laptop so we could see the images once they were taken. Four minutes later we had a diagnosis.

"You're having an aortic dissection," I said. "The tearing feeling that you're sensing is exactly what's going on. The aorta, the major blood vessel in the chest, has torn. From your high blood pressure and from the stress of lifting the piano."

"So what does all that mean in English?"

"It means we have to get you to the hospital right now. It means you're going to end up in the operating room to fix this as quickly as we can get you there."

"Operation?"

"You don't have much choice."

"Even if I'm feeling better?"

"Are you?"

"A lot. The pain is much better. I'm not as short of breath."

He did look better. More color in his face, his breathing easier, and even his sweating had decreased.

"That's from the medicines we gave you," I said. "The morphine is helping with the pain and the other medicines have lowered your blood pressure, but the damage has been done and it needs to be fixed."

"Should I call the medics?" Nathan asked.

"No. He needs to get there now. We'll call in a medevac helicopter."

"I'm on it," Divya said. She pulled out her cell phone.

"Or you can use mine," Nathan said.

"Yours isn't equipped for this."

"I assume time is important here?" Nathan asked.

I nodded.

"Then mine is better. It's here, right out back, and I can have my pilot ready to go in five minutes. Mine's faster anyway. We can be at Hamptons Heritage before the medic chopper even gets here."

A dilemma. Speed or better equipment? I opted for the former.

"Okay, let's do it."

Todd nodded and snapped open his cell phone.

"Is there someone I should call?" I asked Jimmy.

"My wife. Her name's Roxanne."

He gave me the number and I punched it into my cell. After she answered, I told her who I was and explained what was going on with her husband, telling her we were flying him to Hamptons Heritage. I then handed the phone to Jimmy so they could talk.

I looked at Divya. "We'll ride with them."

"Helicopter will be ready in five," Todd said as he closed his cell phone.

"Do you have something we can move him on?" I asked Nathan.

"Like what?"

"A stretcher would be nice, but a wide board or something like that will do."

He thought for a minute and then slowly shook his head. "Don't have either of those."

"A lounge chair will work," I said. "One of the ones by the pool."

Nathan snapped a finger and two of the workers headed toward the back.

I began reexamining Jimmy while Divya ran out to the van to restock our crash kit. Evan was in another world. I could hear him and Nathan talking while I worked.

"This looks so cool," Evan said. "It's like a presidential inauguration."

"Presidential is what we're going for," Nathan said. "When the room is filled with people in their colonial attire it should look like an inauguration."

"Which brings up a question," Evan said. "About costumes."

Good grief.

"What costumes?" Nathan asked.

"I couldn't decide what to be," Evan said. "What do you think?"

Nathan eyed him. "Maybe a banker or a silversmith. Or I think a bookkeeper would be perfect."

"Why does everyone keep saying that? Is it because I'm an accountant?"

"No," Nathan said. "It's because you look smart. Bookish."

"You think so?" Evan asked. "Not like a superspy?"

Nathan studied Evan for a minute and then shook his head. "I'd go with bookkeeper."

One of the workers walked up. "Mr. Zimmer, should we go ahead and move the piano?"

"Sure."

The man nodded, and he and three of his coworkers began rolling the huge Steinway out of the room.

"It's beautiful," Evan said.

"It was a gift," Todd said. "From Van Cliburn."

"*The* Van Cliburn?"

Nathan shrugged. "A guy I did business with— actually a guy who invested with me—was a friend of Mr. Cliburn's. I offered him some free advice. On a couple of investments. It worked out. This was his thanks." Nathan waved a hand toward the piano.

"Do you play?" Evan asked.

"When I was younger. Too busy now."

"Which is unfortunate," Todd said. "He's very good."

"Maybe at one time, but not so much now."

"Isn't it like riding a bicycle?" Evan asked. "Once you know how to do it you can do it forever?"

"Perhaps, but that doesn't qualify you for the Tour

de France. The piano is the same way. I can still play, just not at the level I would like."

Divya returned with the restocked crash kit just as two of the workers appeared with a lounge chair. Divya and I hooked Jimmy up to our portable cardiac monitor and then settled him on the chair. Four workers carried him and his makeshift stretcher to the helicopter pad, a hundred yards away. The copter's rotors were spinning, the pilot busy with his instruments. We loaded Jimmy through the side door.

The helicopter was large and plush. The passenger area probably held a dozen people. A row of dark brown leather captain's seats stretched along one side and a matching bench seat along the other. We set the stretcher on the bench and strapped it in with a pair of the seat belts. Divya rechecked Jimmy's blood pressure while I adjusted his IV.

"Blood pressure is still good," Divya said.

"How's the discomfort?" I asked.

"Better."

"You guys ready?" the pilot asked.

"Yeah."

We buckled ourselves into a pair of the captain's chairs and held on as the copter jerked skyward. I looked out the window toward Nathan, Todd, and Evan, who stood watching, each shielding his eyes from the rotor blast. They rapidly shrank as the copter nosed up, turned out over the ocean, gained more altitude, and whipped around, aiming for Hamptons Heritage.

Nathan was right. His copter was fast. Very fast. It seemed to take only a minute to gain altitude and reach cruising speed.

We learned that the pilot's name was Vinnie Conner. Call sign Con-Man. A former marine copter pilot who had seen duty in both Iraq and Afghanistan.

"This baby's a Sikorsky S-seventy-six. Top of the line. She'll do about one-seventy. We should be there in no time."

I watched the terrain whip by below. Once we settled into straight-line flight I unbuckled my belt and reexamined Jimmy. He was lethargic and poorly responsive to my questions. His pupils were small and poorly reactive from the morphine. His blood pressure was now low. Too low. Seventy over forty.

Divya mixed up a Dobutamine drip and I plugged it into his IV.

"Jimmy? Look at me."

His eyes fluttered open and he looked toward the ceiling, unfocused.

"Jimmy?"

He jerked in a deep breath and then his gaze landed on me. "Doc? How am I doing?"

"Blood pressure's up to one-oh-five," Divya said.

"Better. Just hang in there, Jimmy. We'll be at the hospital shortly."

"Never been in a helicopter before," Jimmy said. "Wish I could see out the window."

I laughed. "Maybe next time."

"ETA is four minutes," Vinnie said. "They'll have a crew waiting on the roof for us."

"You sound like you've done this before," I said.

"After the Marines, I flew a medevac copter for a while. Out on the West Coast. That's what I was doing when Nathan hired me."

"You like this better?"

"Who wouldn't? This Sikorsky is a great rig, Nathan is an easy boss, and the pay is off the charts. Not to mention some pretty nice digs."

"I take it you live on the property?" Divya asked.

"One of the guesthouses is part of the deal." He raised a hand and then spoke into the mouthpiece of his headset. "Three minutes. We're passing over the freeway right now." He listened a beat and then, "Roger that."

"Roger that," Jimmy said and then he laughed.

Morphine is a great drug. It'll make you giddy in even the direst of situations.

The freeway, packed with traffic, slid by beneath us. Good thing we took the air route. Wouldn't want to be sitting in that. The copter now began to rock and bounce.

Turning his head toward us, Vinnie said, "There's always a bit of wind with these rooftop landings."

"Roger that," Jimmy said and giggled again. "Roger that, Roger."

"You guys might want to make sure he's secure and then buckle up again. It can get a little rough."

We did. It was.

The copter pitched and yawed, but Vinnie handled it like a master. My heart not so well. It seemed to take refuge in my throat. Finally I felt the runners contact the roof and the engine drop to idle. I realized I'd been holding my breath and exhaled loudly. Through the window three men and a woman, each wearing dark blue surgical scrubs beneath white coats, ran toward us, a stretcher in tow.

When I stepped out of the copter, I saw that one of the white-coated men was Dr. Lloyd Baransky, Hamptons Heritage's best cardiovascular surgeon.

The other two men moved Jimmy from the lounge chair to a real stretcher, the woman holding the IV bag in one hand and our cardiac monitor in the other. They headed toward the entry door.

Dr. Baransky, Divya, and I followed.

"I understand it's an aortic dissection?" Baransky asked.

I went through the story with him as we followed the stretcher into the pre-op holding area.

"Let's get a CBC, SMA Twenty, PT, PTT, and type and cross for eight units stat," Baransky said. "EKG and chest X-ray, too."

The nurses transferred Jimmy to a bed and switched his leads over to their monitor. Divya took our portable unit and set it on the floor beside our crash kit.

I removed my laptop from my bag and popped it open. "Here's the X-ray we took twenty-five minutes ago." The image appeared on the screen.

Baransky slipped on a pair of half-glasses and studied it. His brow furrowed. "Based on the mediastinal shadow, it looks like a Type One. Guess that rules out an endovascular approach."

Aortic dissections—tears and rips in the aorta—are of three basic classifications. Type 2 involves the part just above the heart, the ascending aorta; Type 3 the descending aorta, the part past where the left subclavian artery branches off and heads toward the arm. Type 1 involves everything. The ascending, the descending, and most important, the aortic arch, the loop in the chest where the carotid arteries that supply blood to the brain come off. By far the most dangerous of the three types.

Endovascular treatment is the placing of a stent in the aorta to repair the tear. Perfect for Type 3 dissections and those involving the abdominal aorta. Not useful for the Type 1 that Jimmy Sutter had. He needed to be opened up. Soon.

"Somebody want to tell me what's going on?" Jimmy asked.

While blood was drawn, X-rays and an EKG taken, that's what Baransky did, even drawing a diagram on the back of Jimmy's medical chart to help explain what had happened and what needed to be done.

"Sounds serious," Jimmy said.

"Very," I said. "But you're in the right place. Dr. Baransky and his team will fix this."

"I owe you, Doc."

"You just get better. I'm going to call your wife again

and let her know we're here and that you're heading for the operating room."

"I know she's freaked out. Tell her to take her time if she's going to drive here."

"Will do."

Chapter 7

With Jimmy Sutter off to the OR, Divya and I headed down to the ER. It was quiet and calm, with only a handful of patients and neither of the major trauma rooms occupied. I remembered days like this from when I ran an ER. Moments like this, when you actually had time to think, were treasured gifts to any ER physician or nurse. Moments when you weren't so swamped with the injured and the ill that sitting down and reflecting was actually possible. Moments when you weren't jumping from crisis to crisis, catastrophe to catastrophe, barely finding time to breathe. These moments never lasted long, but they were always a welcome respite.

We each made a few calls, one of mine to Jimmy's wife. I told her Jimmy was on his way to surgery and that Dr. Baransky would talk with her as soon as he finished.

"How long does this type of surgery take?" she asked.

"Hours," I said. "Could be five or six or could be twelve."

"Twelve? Is it that serious?"

"Very. It's a complex surgery and takes time."

"Is he going to be okay?"

"He's in good hands. He'll do just fine."

I left it at that. I didn't want to tell her that the mortality associated with this type of dissection was not a small number. She didn't need to hear that right now. She needed comforting. She needed not to panic. After she promised to take her time driving over, I hung up.

Finally, Evan arrived in the HankMed van. Divya and I dropped him at Shadow Pond and headed out to do the follow-up visits we had delayed due to Jimmy's emergency.

Divya and I made it back to Shadow Pond just before six p.m. Divya packed up our computers and went inside while I restocked the emergency kit from the supplies in the back of the HankMed van. Just as I closed the rear and clicked the lock, Jill pulled up. I held her car door and she stepped out, purse over her shoulder, bottle of wine in her hand.

"I was hoping you'd make it back in time for dinner," she said. "How's your patient doing?"

"He's in surgery. It'll be a long one so I don't expect to hear anything until very late tonight or more likely tomorrow."

"I heard Dr. Baransky is doing the surgery."

"That's right."

"He's one of the best, so it should go well."

"As well as this type of surgery can go."

"A bad one?"

"The worst. Any aortic dissection is tricky, but the one Jimmy Sutter has is at the high end of tricky."

Jill's gaze settled beyond my right shoulder. I turned to see Boris's Bentley moving up the drive toward where we stood.

Jill and Boris had at one time had a strained relationship. Boris had given a very generous donation to Jill's community clinic. An anonymous donation. Something the very private Boris Kuester von Jurgens-Ratenicz takes seriously. Jill had mistakenly leaked his name in an attempt to garner more donors and word filtered to Boris. He felt Jill had betrayed his trust, which of course she had. She apologized, Boris accepted, and now all was back in balance.

Dieter parked next to the HankMed van and Boris climbed from the backseat.

"How is your patient doing?" he asked me.

It never failed to amaze me how Boris seemed to know things. Like he had a fly on every wall in the Hamptons. Who knows, maybe he did.

"You heard about that," I said, more a statement than a question.

He shrugged.

"He's in surgery, so we'll see."

He turned to Jill. "And you, Miss Casey? I imagine you're quite busy with your health fair preparations, no?"

"There's a lot to do."

"And your fund-raising? Has it gone well?"

"Very. We're ahead of our goal."

"Excellent." He hesitated for a beat. "Perhaps I could help? If it isn't too late."

"It's never too late for donations." She stopped suddenly, eyes wide. "I'm sorry. I assumed that's what you meant?"

Boris gave a curt nod. "That's exactly what I meant. I'll have Dieter bring a check around."

"That's very kind of you."

"Anonymous, no?"

"You can count on it."

"I do." He nodded toward the bottle of wine. "And perhaps a second bottle of wine."

"That's not necessary," I said.

He casually waved a hand. "Something that will go with the excellent meal Evan is preparing."

Boris nodded again, turned, and walked toward the front door. Dieter gave a half bow and followed.

I watched them go while wondering how Boris could know what Evan was making. If he did, that is. But if he didn't, how would he know which wine to select?

Boris the enigma.

Even I didn't know what Evan had planned. I wasn't sure Evan did. I think more often than not he simply opened the fridge and threw together whatever was in there. Usually not much. But somehow he always seemed to make it work.

My brother the chef.

"What was that all about?" Jill asked.

"I guess he wants us to have an expensive wine with our dinner."

"Not that. I was talking about his offer to donate money to the health fair."

"It's just Boris being Boris," I said. "You know he's always giving money in situations like this."

"I know. But I didn't ask him for money."

"Maybe Evan did."

"Maybe. Anyway it's very generous of him to offer."

"Like I said, Boris being Boris."

"Have you talked to Boris recently?" I asked Evan as I walked into the kitchen.

Evan stood at the stove, spoon in his hand, wearing a dark green apron that said KISS THE COOK in white lettering.

"No. Why?"

"He just offered Jill a donation for the fair and I thought maybe you had talked with him about it."

"Nope."

"So how did he know we were gathering donations?" Jill asked.

"Because Boris knows everything," Evan said.

I shrugged. "It does seem that way."

"He'd make a good spy," Evan said. "Like me."

I let the editorial comment slide and said, "Maybe Boris is a spy."

Evan stopped and stared at me. "You think so? That

would be so cool." He looked at Divya. "Make a note to ask him."

"I think not," Divya said.

"Why not?"

"Because what Boris is or isn't is none of your concern."

"But us spies have to stick together."

My brother's delusions know no bounds. I started to point that out but instead said, "I think most real spies don't advertise the fact that they're spies."

"Unlike you," Divya said to Evan.

Evan shook his head but somehow managed to stifle any retort.

Jill placed the wine on the table. "What are you making? It smells delicious."

Evan ran through the menu.

While Divya and I were seeing our follow-ups, Evan had finally settled on what to cook for dinner. He had apparently gotten the 1776 theme in his head and decided to make a Williamsburg dinner.

I couldn't help but think part of his culinary decision was a remnant of the trip we had taken to Williamsburg when we were kids. Evan had been fascinated with all the workshops—the blacksmith, the tailor, and the glassblowers, but mostly the bread makers. We had stayed in a small off-the-beaten-path bed-and-breakfast with our dad and had dinner at one of the colonial taverns. That was where Evan was introduced to Sally Lunn bread. He obsessed about that for at least a year.

So tonight he decided to make roast chicken breast, apple-and-cranberry cornbread stuffing, stewed apples, and of course Sally Lunn bread. The aroma of the baking bread made my stomach growl.

"I think I like this new domestic side of you," I said to Evan.

"What domestic side? Just because I like to cook?"

Jill opened the wine and poured four glasses. She asked Evan if she could help, but he said he had everything under control, so she, Divya, and I sat at the counter and watched him finish things up.

"I got a brief break today and went by a cool costume shop," Jill said. "They have some pretty amazing stuff."

"Any bookkeeper outfits?" I asked.

Evan turned, glared at me, and then returned to stirring the pot of simmering apples.

Jill laughed. "Didn't see any of those. But I did like their highwayman outfits. That might be pretty cool for us." She looked at me.

"Maybe that would be better for Evan," Divya said. "After all, he's the money man."

Evan turned and looked at her. "Somehow I don't see the CFO of HankMed dressed as a highwayman. It might send the wrong message."

"Perhaps. But for you it would be perfect."

"But I'm a spy. That's so much cooler than being a robber."

"And of course you are a superspy," Divya said.

Evan looked toward where his cell phone lay beneath the lamp next to the sofa and took a step in that direction.

Divya stopped him by saying, "Don't you dare."

Evan shrugged. "Not necessary anyway. Everyone knows that Evan R. Lawson is a superspy."

"And a modest one," Divya fired back.

"Who got the critical information from StellarCare?" Evan asked.

Evan never lets go of his victories, big or little. He holds on to them forever. I guess we all do that; Evan just does it with passion. The truth was that he did indeed get the crucial information we needed to resolve the Julian Morelli affair.

Divya rolled her eyes. "You did."

"Yes, I did." Evan began spooning the stuffing and the apples into serving bowls. "Dinnertime."

Jill helped Evan carry the serving dishes to the table and we all sat.

Evan had outdone himself. The chicken was perfect, the apples sweet and rich, and the Sally Lunn bread light and yeasty.

"Excellent," I said.

"Maybe you should go as a baker?" Divya said.

"And what would you be? A tavern wench?"

"Not likely." She took a bite of stuffing. "What would a baker wear?"

"An apron," I said. "Just not one that says 'Kiss the cook.'"

"Maybe a puffy hat," Jill added.

"Did they wear puffy hats back then?" Divya asked.

Evan hesitated a beat as if considering that and then shook his head. "No, I should be a spy."

"Maybe a baker-spy," Divya said. "You could wear the hat and a cape and steal recipes."

Everyone laughed.

"Maybe we should consider the highwayman thing," Jill said to me. "It might not be good for a CFO but for a CEO it would fit."

"Are you saying I'm a robber baron?"

She laughed. "No. But it still might be fun."

I thought about that for a minute. It beat any idea that I had come up with, which of course was no idea at all. "What exactly did highwaymen wear?"

"The outfits they had at the store had long shirts, a wide leather belt, and capes. Oh, and a fake pistol you could stuff beneath the belt."

"Where is this place?" I asked.

"Over toward Montauk. Want to swing by and see what they look like?" Jill asked.

"Tomorrow?"

"We probably should. We only have a few days to come up with something."

"Maybe after our first patient tomorrow?" Divya said.

"Sure," I said. "We could be there about nine."

Jill pulled her phone from her purse and worked its keyboard. "Looks like that'll work. I have an eight o'clock meeting and then I was going over to the high school to see how the preparations are going. I'll meet you there in between."

"Then maybe we'll follow you to the school," Divya said, and then to me, "We need to take another look at our booth and decide how we're going to set it up."

I forked a piece of chicken. "Sounds like a plan."

Conversation ended for a few minutes as everyone enjoyed the meal. The silence was broken by a knock at the door. When I opened it, Dieter looked at me. He extended both hands. One held a check, the other a bottle of wine.

I took them both and said, "Want to come in?"

"No. Boris wanted you to have the check this evening and, of course, the wine."

"That's very kind of him. Tell him we are grateful."

Dieter gave a mechanical smile and a slight bow. "Then I'm off." He turned and walked away. Just like that.

I placed the wine on the table. The label said it was a 2000 Château Latour Pauillac. I assumed it was good, and expensive, but my knowledge of wine is near zero.

"What's that?" Evan asked, picking up the bottle.

"A gift from Boris."

Evan studied the label. "Dude, this is expensive."

Jill looked at it. "Wow. This is the good stuff."

"What's with Boris being so generous?" Evan asked.

"He's always generous," I said.

"I'll open it," Divya said. She stood and walked to the counter where the opener lay.

"That's not the half of it," I said. I handed the check to Jill.

She looked at it, then up at me, and then back to the check. "Are you kidding?"

Evan snatched it. "Let me see." He looked at it, his eyes widening. "Dude, this is serious coin."

"That's Boris," I said. "He doesn't do anything half-way."

Divya returned with the wine and four fresh glasses and sat. Evan handed her the check. "Oh, my, this is serious." She gave the check back to Jill.

"Adding this to the great job Evan has done puts us way over the top," Jill said.

"That's Evan R. Lawson, fund-raiser extraordinaire."

"Your business card is getting quite cluttered," Divya said.

"How so?"

"Let's see—superspy, master chef, and now fund-raiser extraordinaire. That's a lot to get on a card."

"Don't forget supercool bon vivant," Evan said.

"How could I forget that?" Divya asked.

We were back to high school again.

I poured wine for everyone. It was fantastic. Way too expensive for my blood, but it was an unexpected treat.

Silence fell again as everyone returned to Evan's wonderful meal. The Sally Lunn bread was exactly as I remembered.

"Evan, you've outdone yourself again," I said. "This bread is outstanding."

"Just like when we were kids," he said.

What'd I tell you?

"Kids?" Jill asked.

Evan related the story of our childhood trip to Williamsburg. I corrected him on a couple of things and he corrected me back, but mostly we agreed.

Chapter 8

Angela Delaney's modest two-bedroom cottage was nestled on the shore of a small pond just off Hands Creek Road a few miles north of East Hampton. It was white with black trim and shutters. Round white posts supported a sloping roof and were connected by intricately patterned black wrought-iron railings. Evan wheeled the HankMed van into the gravel parking area that ran along one side of the house and we climbed out. I hoisted our medical bag over one shoulder while Divya grabbed her purse and laptop.

The morning was warm, with a slight breeze rustling the trees that shaded the house. We found Angela on her back porch, sitting in one of the two rockers that faced the pond. She looked up from the book she was reading and smiled.

"How wonderful," she said, setting the book on the small round table next to her. "I get to see all of you today."

Angela had suffered a hip fracture two weeks earlier and had undergone a total hip replacement. A THR in medical jargon. After four days in the hospital and ten days in rehab, her orthopedist had discharged her yesterday afternoon.

We climbed the three steps to the porch.

"You look wonderful," I said.

"Liar."

"No, you truly do," Divya said.

"I haven't washed my hair in days and haven't put on any makeup in two weeks."

"Must be your natural beauty," I said.

She laughed. "Now that's what I call bedside manner."

"Happy to be home?" I asked.

"My favorite place in the world." She waved a hand toward the pond. "When I die this is where I want to be. Sitting right here. Listening to my birds and frogs and insects."

The pond was peaceful. The way I imagined Walden Pond would be, though I knew Walden was much larger and now a tourist area. Complete with swimming and a gift shop. But this little pond with its mirrored green surface, hardy reeds, and tree-shaded banks must be what Thoreau saw in his mind's eye when he wrote about it.

"I can understand that." I sat in the rocker next to her, tilting forward, resting my elbows on my knees. "How are you doing?"

"Fine. Still a little sore, but I'm up and around."

"Did your granddaughter come?"

"Oh, yes. I hate to drag her away from her busy life, but she insisted."

"You'll need some help for a while. Knowing you, not long, but a few weeks anyway."

"I'm old, not an invalid."

"And you shouldn't be alone while you're getting back on your feet."

"The physical therapy folks will be coming out every day. That's enough company."

"Don't go all little-old-lady cranky on me."

"At my age I can do what I want." She gave me one of her mischievous smiles.

"Are you doing your exercises?"

She extended her leg, twisted it one way and then the other. "See. It works fine. And I use those rubber-band things they gave me three times a day just like I did in rehab."

I slid from the rocker and knelt in front of her. "Let me see." I grasped her ankle and knee, flexing her knee and then her hip to about forty-five degrees. A little stiff. "Does that hurt?"

"Not at all."

"What about this?" I rotated her knee inward slightly and then outward, checking the stability and mobility of her new hip.

"A little." She smiled. "But you're much more gentle than those physical therapy folks." She shook her head. "They're a tough crew."

"It's for your own good."

"That's what they keep telling me." She flashed a smile. "I don't believe them either."

I eased her leg down until her foot rested on the porch again. "Looks like they're doing a good job. You'll be dancing before you know it."

"Are you asking me for a date?" she asked, a wicked glint in her eyes.

"I see the new hip didn't change you a bit."

"Did you expect it would? They didn't operate on my brain."

I heard car tires on gravel and looked up as an SUV pulled in and parked near the back edge of the lot, nosing up beneath an overhanging cedar branch. A tall, lean, deeply tanned blond woman stepped out. She grabbed a bag of groceries and headed our way.

"There she is now," Angela said.

She introduced us to Danielle, her granddaughter.

"How's she doing?" Danielle asked.

"Great," I said. "As expected."

"She is tough."

I laughed. "That she is."

"You guys sound like I'm shoe leather," Angela said.

"Much tougher than that," Danielle said.

Angela was tough. One of those seventy-five-year-olds that you just knew would see a hundred. Last year she had gone through a rocky gall bladder surgery. One that would have knocked most people down for a while. But despite the infection that had spread throughout her bloodstream, Angela snapped back like a twenty-year-old. Two weeks after the surgery you couldn't tell anything had happened to her.

"Let me put these away." Danielle started toward the back door. "Can I get you guys anything? Maybe some juice or a cola?"

"We're fine," I said.

She nodded and disappeared inside.

"Isn't she lovely?" Angela asked.

"She is," I said.

"She lives out in LA. She's a world-class surfer. Won all kinds of awards and contests. All over the world."

"Really?" Evan said, his gaze turning toward the back door as if looking for Danielle.

"Oh, yes. She's been on the cover of about every surfing magazine there is. I have a whole stack of them."

"I'd like to see them," Evan said.

Of course he would.

"See them what?" Danielle had returned.

"Your magazine covers, dear."

Danielle blushed and rolled her eyes. "Grandma, don't embarrass me."

"Wouldn't dream of it." Another devilish grin from Angela.

"Have you been surfing long?" Divya asked.

"I've been on a board since I was five."

"I hear you're pretty good," I said, nodding toward Angela.

"Grandma exaggerates, but I do okay."

"She's won dozens of meets and ranked . . . What is it now?"

"Sixth."

"Sixth in the world," Angela said. "I'd say that's good."

"Wow," Evan said. "A real pro surfer. That's so cool."

"Do any of you surf?" Danielle asked.

"Not me," Divya said. "I'm not big on water."

"I tried it once," Evan said. "Didn't work out so well. I think the waves were too big that day."

"Three feet?" I said.

"They look bigger when you're in them," Evan said.

Danielle laughed. "Yes, they do."

"What's it like out there?" Divya asked. "When you're riding a wave?"

"Exhilarating. You feel so free. Like you're flying."

"Right up until you crash. Right?" I said.

She laughed again. "True. Sometimes it can be a real washing machine if you get thrashed by a big wave."

"Has that ever happened to you?" Divya asked.

"It's happened to every surfer. Sometimes you slam the bottom and get rolled over rocks. Sand up your nose. Tumbling around like a rag doll. Can't tell up from down. Sometimes you think you'll never find the surface."

"Sounds scary to me," I said.

"But when you're flying along over the water?" She shrugged. "There's nothing quite like it."

"Teach me," Evan said.

"Teach you to surf?" Divya said. "That's a disaster in the making."

"Why would you say that?"

"Coordination isn't your strong suit."

"Ignore her," Evan said. "I'll even pay you."

Danielle laughed. "That wouldn't be necessary. But I need to stay here with Grandma."

"No, you don't," Angela said. "I'm perfectly capable of puttering around here on my own. Besides, I'd bet Evan would be good at it."

Evan's chest puffed out. "See. Angela thinks I could do it."

"She obviously hasn't been around you much," Divya said.

Angela laughed and then said to Danielle, "Go ahead. I'll be fine."

"You sure?"

"Of course."

Danielle hesitated and then said, "Okay. But I should warn you, the waves here aren't very big, so we might not be able to find any to ride."

"I think smaller is better," I said. "Otherwise Evan might be joining Angela with her physical therapy."

"Are you saying I might break something?"

"Or someone," Divya said.

"Maybe around three or four?" Danielle said. "While Grandma is taking her nap?"

"That'll work," Evan said.

"Great. I'll meet you at the beach. Near that seafood restaurant."

"Panama Joe's?"

"That's it. There's a parking lot right next to it."

"I'll be there." Evan clapped his hands. "This is going to be so cool."

Cool was definitely not the word that came to mind.

Chapter 9

We got as far as the parking area before my cell phone buzzed. I didn't recognize the number. I answered and found it was Dr. Lloyd Baransky.

"I wanted to give you an update on your patient Jimmy Sutter," Baransky said. "I would have called last night, but we didn't complete his surgery until nearly two a.m. It was a tough one."

"How so?"

"The dissection involved both carotids and the left subclavian."

"Not good."

"No. But all went well. Just took time."

"So he's okay?"

"Amazingly so. Still on the vent, but making urine and his renal and cardiac parameters are perfect. He's coming around and moving all extremities. We'll likely extubate him soon and then we'll have a better handle on his neuro status, but so far it looks good."

As soon as I hung up I told Divya what Baransky had said.

"He's a lucky man," she said.

"Very."

We climbed in the van and Evan cranked it up. My cell buzzed again. This number I recognized. It was Jill. She said she was running late and asked if we could meet at the costume shop a little later. No problem. So we headed back to Shadow Pond, where Divya and I settled at the patio table, laptops open, and began working on patient files.

No easy task with Evan's constant interruptions.

If deciding on a Fourth of July costume was hard, choosing a bathing suit for surfing was impossible. He popped in and out of the house, a new suit on each time. I had no idea he owned that many.

"What do you think of these?" Evan asked as he came back outside. He now wore a pair of dark blue swim trunks.

"They're fine," I said.

"You didn't even look at them."

I looked at them. "They're fine."

Evan tugged at the waistband. "What I need are some cool baggies like they wear on TV."

"What TV would that be?" I asked. "Don't know that I've seen baggies in quite a while."

"Not since Gidget," Divya said.

"You weren't even born when Gidget surfed," Evan said.

"Neither were you, but I watch old movies, too."

"I don't think Gidget actually surfed," I said. "I don't remember ever seeing her with wet hair."

"But she sat on the beach and looked cool," Evan said. "Or was it hot?"

"Perhaps that's what you should do," Divya said. "Sit on the beach. But you looking cool—or hot—is out of the question."

He shook his head and headed back inside.

Divya glanced at her watch. "Are you almost done?"

"Just a couple more charts to complete."

"We have to meet Jill in half an hour."

"We'll make it."

Evan returned, wearing bright yellow elastic bicycle pants. "What about these?"

"The sharks will have no problem finding you," I said.

"Sharks? There aren't any sharks around here."

"The ocean doesn't have compartments," I said. "They can go wherever they want."

"That's true," Divya said. "And they love surfers."

I nodded. "Something about them looking like seals from below."

"That's a myth," Evan said. "Shark attacks on surfers are rare."

"True," I said. "But the problem with statistics is that they're for the masses. For the individual it's either zero or one hundred percent."

"I'll take zero, then."

"I'm not sure the statistics god gives you a choice," Divya said.

"Evan R. Lawson is not afraid." He went back into the house.

As soon as the door closed, my cell phone chimed. It was Jill.

"You guys ready to head over?" she asked.

"As soon as we dress Evan."

"Dress Evan?"

"He's been prancing around in bathing suits for the past half hour."

"This should be good. Exactly why is he wearing a bathing suit?"

"He's set up a surfing lesson for this afternoon."

"Surfing? Evan?"

"That would be the one."

"You're kidding."

"Wish I was."

"Who on earth would agree to give Evan surfing lessons?"

"Someone with a death wish."

Jill laughed.

I told her about Danielle Delaney.

"Really? Danielle Delaney? She's like a world-class surfer."

"You know who she is?"

"Of course. One of the world's hottest female athletes."

"She is that."

"Should I be jealous?"

"That would be nice."

"Funny. How did Evan pull this off?"

"Danielle's grandmother is a patient. We saw her this morning and, well, you know Evan."

"True."

"Right now he's trying to decide what suit to wear."

"What difference does it make? He'll be wearing a wet suit."

"That's true," I said. "I never thought of that."

I wished I had thought of that. It might have saved Divya and me a lot of aggravation. Wait—what was I thinking? No it wouldn't. Evan would simply have obsessed about the wet suit.

Evan came out the door as Jill asked, "Does he have a wet suit?"

"I'll let you ask him." I handed the phone to Evan. "Jill has some thoughts on your surfing safari."

Evan took the phone. His side of the conversation went like this:

"Yes, that Danielle Delaney."

"She wants to. Even volunteered to."

"Around four."

"No, I don't have a wet suit. Why would I need one?"

"It's not that cold."

"Really? It's July. I thought the water would be warmer."

"Okay."

He hung up.

"What's the story?" I asked.

"I need to rent a wet suit."

I closed my laptop and stood. "First let's meet Jill at the costume shop."

The trip to the costume shop should have been easy. A quick in and out. Jill, Divya, and I could have selected a costume and been out the door in no time. One problem. Evan. His decision-making abilities were anemic at best.

As soon as I walked in the door I realized I'd never been to a costume store. Maybe when I was very young, but if so I didn't remember it. And I would have remembered something like Marie's Costume and Theatrical Wear Emporium. No cheap plastic Superman or Batman costumes. No cowboys and Indians. No Darth Vader or stormtrooper getups. Marie's looked like the wardrobe department of a Hollywood production company.

The place was huge, warehouselike, with exposed beams, pipes, and conduits crisscrossing the high ceiling and row after row of racks stuffed with clothing. Ball gowns and ballet outfits. Peasant dresses and royal finery. A military row that had everything from Civil War uniforms to full-on Navy Seal gear. And a row of colonial clothing.

We waited at the counter while the woman behind it completed a phone conversation by telling the person on the other end that she did indeed have a selection of Romeo and Juliet outfits and that she would be open until six. She hung up and smiled.

"Can I help you?"

"This place is amazing," I said. "I had no idea all this would be here."

She smiled. "We supply several local theaters as well as rent costuming to the public. I'm Marie Santos."

"The owner, I take it?"

"And chief cook and bottle washer."

As I introduced her to Divya and Evan, Jill came through the front door, cell phone to her ear. She immediately ended her call and I introduced her to Marie.

"We need costumes," Evan said.

"I assumed that's why you were here." She flashed a playful smile.

She was in her mid-forties, with dark hair lightly streaked with gray and dark brown eyes that lit up when she smiled.

"What type of costumes?"

"Colonial. Revolutionary War," Jill said.

"Ah." She nodded. "You must be going to Nathan Zimmer's party?"

"Yes, we are," I said. "How'd you know?"

"You're about the two-dozenth persons to come looking for that period. A little unusual in July. Around Halloween I wouldn't have noticed, but July isn't a big month for costumes. Except for the theaters."

"Are we too late?" Evan asked. "Are all the colonial ones gone?"

She waved a hand toward the packed racks. "I think we can find something for you. What did you have in mind?"

"A spy outfit," Evan said. "I want to go as a spy."

"Very good. You'll make a great spy."

Evan looked at me. "See? Not everyone thinks I look like a bookkeeper."

"Marie doesn't know you."

"Actually, you'd make an excellent bookkeeper or newspaperman," Marie said. "I can see you with a blousy shirt, armbands, wire-rimmed glasses, and an eyeshade."

"Sounds like a riverboat gambler," Jill said. "Did they have those in colonial times?"

"I think that was a little later," Marie said. "After the Mississippi River Valley was more populated."

Jill nodded. "That makes sense." She looked at Evan. "So, spy it is."

Marie came around the counter. "This way."

For the next twenty minutes she showed Evan a selection of Revolutionary War spy costumes complete with waistcoats, capes, and hats. While she occupied Evan, Jill and I rummaged through the adjacent racks and Divya moved two rows away to a collection of colonial ball gowns. Finally, Evan, his arms loaded with choices, headed toward the dressing rooms along the back wall.

"Now, what can I help you two with?" Marie asked as she walked to where Jill and I were sorting through one of the racks.

Jill held a Martha Washington dress against her body. Black with white lace at the neck and sleeves. "What about this?"

"Better than a highway robber," I said.

Marie gave us a quizzical look.

"That was one of the things we were considering," I said.

"This is much better," Marie said. "Don't you think?"

"Looks great to me," I said.

"I agree," Marie added. She adjusted the lace at the neckline. "You'll look like a true colonial woman."

"What about him?" Jill nodded in my direction.

Marie studied me for a moment, her brow furrowed, and then said, "Since highwayman is out, I think a frontiersman would work." She turned and headed down the row. We followed.

She shuffled through the hangers until she found the one she was looking for. She removed it and laid it on top of the rack. The costume consisted of a buckskin shirt and pants and a wide leather belt. She slid the shirt from the hanger and, holding it by the shoulders, draped it against my chest. It was medium brown, long, hanging to midthigh, and had fringe across the chest and at the cuffs and hem.

"I think this will work," Marie said.

"I love it," Jill said. "You look like Davy Crockett."

"He wasn't born until after the Revolution. He died at the Alamo in eighteen thirty-six," I said.

"You're just full of worthless information, aren't you?" Jill said.

Marie laughed. "But this was typical frontier wear for eighteenth-century America."

"Do you have a coonskin cap?" Jill asked.

"Yes."

"The outfit is fine, but no coonskin," I said.

"But you'd look so cute in it." Jill laughed.

"Cute is not what I'm going for."

Divya walked up. She was stunning in a rose-colored floor-length gown. A fitted bodice, narrow waist, and broad, flowing skirt. The shoulders bloused and the sleeves flared into lace ruffles.

"Wow!" I said.

"That is stunning," Jill said.

"You don't think it's too much?" Divya asked.

"No," Jill and I said in unison.

"It's perfect," Jill said.

Divya did a full turn. The skirt rustled. "I feel like a true colonial lady."

"That color is perfect for you," Marie said.

Evan came out of the dressing room. He wore brown pants stuffed into knee-high boots, a frilly white shirt beneath a dark brown waistcoat, a wide leather belt with a brass buckle, and a chocolate-colored cape.

"What do you think?" he asked.

"I still think bookkeeper would be more fitting," Divya said.

"And I was just going to say how beautiful you look in that gown," Evan said.

"Thank you." Divya curtsied. "And you make a beautiful spy."

That drew a laugh from Marie.

"Spies aren't beautiful," Evan said. "They're stealthy and cool."

"That's you. Stealthy and cool."

"Absolutely," Evan said as he made a wide turn, causing the cape to flare around him.

Divya raised an eyebrow but said nothing.

"I think our work here is done," I said to Marie.

Chapter 10

Divya and I found ourselves back at the Sag Harbor home of Felicia Hecht. We had intended to head over to the high school, but Felicia had called as we left the costume shop. Her headaches had worsened. We dropped Evan at Shadow Pond and drove up.

"What's going on?" I asked as she directed us into her living room.

"Last night was a tough one. I was up and down all night."

"With the headaches?"

She nodded. "But they're a little different now."

Felicia sat on the sofa and I settled next to her, automatically reaching for her wrist to check her pulse. Steady but fast.

"In what way?"

"This is going to sound odd."

"It's okay," Divya said as she sat in the chair across from the sofa. "We hear odd all the time."

"My tongue felt like it was on fire." She took a deep breath and let it out slowly. "Isn't that crazy?"

"Unusual but not crazy," I said. "Was this with the headaches or at some other time?"

"With. As I said, the headaches were worse last night. I took the pills you gave me and they helped some, but the headaches always came back. Then this morning I felt better. Tired but pain free."

"And then?" I anticipated there was more to the story.

"A couple of hours ago the pain came back. I tried to ride it out, but when my tongue, neck, and right ear started burning, I got worried."

"Only on the right side?" Divya asked.

She nodded.

"What were you doing when it started?" I asked.

"I was talking on the phone with a friend."

"Stressful?"

"Not at all. We were talking about a dinner party we're going to this weekend."

"Let me check things again," I said.

I twisted to face her and again did a brief neurological exam and again felt along the right side of her face and jaw. Nothing. Her neuro exam was still normal and I found no tender areas.

"And I almost fainted," Felicia said.

"When?"

"Just after I called you. I was eating some peanut

butter and crackers. I thought maybe my blood sugar was low or something."

"Did it help? The crackers?"

She shook her head. "Then I felt light-headed. I left the kitchen and headed in here to lie down, but I almost didn't make it. My legs felt rubbery and things looked dim."

"Did you fall?" Divya asked

"No. I made it to the sofa. Once I lay down for a couple of minutes I felt fine."

"Is this the only time that's happened?"

She gave me a sheepish look. "A couple of other times. Last week."

"You didn't tell me that yesterday."

"I know. I'm sorry."

"You have to tell me everything. Okay?"

She nodded. "I promise."

Withholding things from your doctor is not as unusual as most people think. Might not sound logical, but it's not uncommon. Some are afraid the doctor will find something terrible if they reveal all their symptoms. Some simply want to cut things short. Get out of the doctor's office and home as soon as possible. Where it's safe. Where bad things can't be uncovered. Some are simply embarrassed by certain symptoms.

"Have you had any chest pain or shortness of breath?" Divya asked.

"No." She looked at me. "What is all this?"

"The labs we drew yesterday are normal. We had them e-mailed to us as we drove over. The best bet is still a migraine syndrome, but there are a couple of other things we have to consider."

"Like?"

"Unusual coronary symptoms."

"By 'coronary' do you mean heart attack or angina or something like that?"

"Yes. Coronary problems don't always cause chest pain. Sometimes it's just shortness of breath, or dizziness, or neck pain."

She sighed. "That's what took my Charles." She nodded toward the photos on the mantel. "Two years ago."

"It's unlikely that that's what's going on," I said. "But we can quickly rule it out."

"How?"

"A stress test."

"So I have to go to the hospital?"

"No. We can do it right here. We have our stress echo equipment outside in the van."

"I'm impressed. Of course, Ellie said I would be."

"We pay her to say nice things." I smiled. "We can set it up right here in the living room if that's okay."

"Sure."

"While we get things ready why don't you change into something more comfortable and put on your walking shoes if you have any."

"I walk almost every day, so I have plenty of that stuff."

Twenty minutes later Felicia had changed clothes and Divya had finished the resting echocardiogram.

Felicia then climbed on the treadmill belt and we began the exercise portion of the test. While she walked, I asked more questions.

"These dizzy spells? Did they only happen while you were having the headaches?"

"Yes." She hesitated for a beat. "Actually the dizziness seems to happen only when the pain is in my jaw and tongue."

"I thought those symptoms were new. Just today."

"Maybe a few times in the last week. But never before that."

The treadmill kicked up its speed and elevation as she entered the second stage of the Bruce Protocol.

"How long do I have to do this?" Felicia asked.

"Until we get your heart rate up to about one-seventy or until you can't do any more, whichever comes first."

"I'd bet on the latter."

She was wrong. She got her heart rate up to one-eighty before I ended the test. Divya completed the postexercise echocardiogram. I then loaded the images onto my laptop and angled the screen slightly toward Felicia so she could see the images.

"These are ultrasound movies of your heart," I said.

"That's it moving there?"

"Sure is."

"Fascinating. What do you see?"

"A completely normal heart."

"Really?"

"Scout's honor."

"Thank goodness."

"Now that we know it's not your heart, you can relax a bit while we finish what we need to do."

"So you still don't know what it is?"

"Patience." I smiled. "We now know what it isn't and that's important. It isn't your heart, so whatever it is, it'll be less sinister than that."

"Sinister?"

"Maybe not the best word. Let's say less threatening."

She nodded. "That's comforting."

"I think it might be a problem with one of the nerves that come from the base of your brain. But like I told you earlier, let's not get too far down that road until we know exactly what we're dealing with."

"What's next? A surgeon to open my head and look around?"

I laughed. "I don't think we have to go quite that far. I'm going to arrange a brain MRI for you over at Hamptons Heritage. Later today. While you're there they'll place a Holter monitor on you. It's a device that records all your heartbeats for twenty-four hours."

"I thought you said my heart was normal."

"It is. But if what I suspect is indeed the problem, slow heart rates and dizziness, even passing out, can be part of it."

"You guys are just full of good news, aren't you?"

I smiled. "We try."

It's not every day that you get a call from the medical examiner. Actually the call didn't come from him. It was from Sergeant McCutcheon. But the medical examiner was sitting right there in McCutcheon's office. McCutcheon wondered if I was available to drop by for a chat. When I asked what it was about he said they would tell me when I got there.

If a call like that doesn't tweak your curiosity you must be in a coma.

I told him I'd be right over.

We still had two follow-up visits scheduled, so Divya dropped me by Shadow Pond to pick up my trusty Saab and she took the HankMed van. We arranged to meet over at the high school after we were finished.

When I entered McCutcheon's office I was greeted by two somber faces. McCutcheon and Suffolk County's medical examiner, Dr. James Hawkins. I had met Hawkins a few months earlier during the StellarCare/ Julian Morelli investigation.

Hawkins stood and shook my hand. "Thanks for coming over."

"Good to see you again."

"Have a seat," McCutcheon said from behind his desk.

Curiosity faded to dread as I sat in one of the two chairs that faced his desk. Hawkins took the other.

"What's this about?" I asked.

McCutcheon nodded to Hawkins.

Hawkins twisted slightly in his chair to face me, one elbow resting on the arm. "Those pills that you got from Kevin Moxley."

I hate it when that little electric current goes up the back of your neck. The one that makes the hair stand on end and drops your body temperature a couple of degrees. The one that says the light at the end of the tunnel is a train. A large, fast-moving train with no brakes.

"Crystal meth?" I asked.

Hawkins nodded. "Yes. They did contain crystal meth. But they also contained another amphetamine. Methylenedioxymethamphetamine. MDMA."

I stared at him for a beat. "Ecstasy?" I glanced at McCutcheon and then back to Hawkins. "They had both crystal meth and ecstasy?"

"Afraid so." He slipped off his glasses, rubbed one eye with a knuckle, and then pinched the bridge of his nose. He looked as if a headache might be brewing. He settled his glasses back in place with a sigh. "Sometimes I don't understand this planet. Why on earth would someone cook up this concoction?"

"Money," McCutcheon said. "It always comes down to the money."

"When I saw Kevin Moxley he certainly behaved and looked as if he was on amphetamines," I said. "I know that ecstasy is an amphetamine, but its major effects are more psychedelic. I didn't see that. Kevin seemed oriented and he certainly understood everything that I said to him."

"That likely has to do with the dosing," Hawkins said. "Those little pink pills were mostly fillers and crystal meth, but there was a very tiny amount of the MDMA."

I thought about that for a minute. "Just enough to add a little euphoria to the speed? Something like that?"

"That's how I see it," Hawkins said.

Methamphetamine alone can create euphoria and hyperactivity. It can also drive your blood pressure and heart rate through the roof and kill you. Happens every day. Toss in a little ecstasy and your brain can get really freaky. Delusions, hallucinations, emotional instability, even seizures. Whoever figured out this combination was trying to get a leg up on the competition by selling a product that had a little more effect. A little more euphoria. And unfortunately, the potential for a little more death.

"Have you ever seen anything like this before?" I asked.

"No," Hawkins said. "I called a couple of my colleagues and neither had they."

I looked at McCutcheon. "What's the plan from here?"

He leaned forward and rested his thick forearms on the edge of his desk. His biceps and shoulders looked as if they might rip the seams of his shirt. "I've issued a department-wide bulletin on the couple Kevin Moxley described. A BOLO. Means 'Be on the Lookout.' I wish we had more to go on, but his description is all we have."

"And their names," I said.

"Probably bogus."

That made sense. If you lived and worked in the

shadows you probably wouldn't use the name on your driver's license.

"How did Kevin hook up with them?" I asked. "I mean, was it random or did he know how to reach them?"

"I asked him the same thing. Seems he actually had a phone number for them."

"That should help."

"Not really. I called the number. Tried to act like a buyer. It didn't go well."

"What happened?"

"The dude asked me how old I was. I told him fifteen. He asked what grade I was in. I told him I was a sophomore. He asked me who my teacher was. I guessed wrong. I only know a handful of teachers over at the high school and apparently the one I chose taught senior classes."

"What happened?"

"He said that I should have a nice day and hung up."

"Can't you trace the phone or something?" I asked.

"I did. It's a prepaid. No way to track it back. He'll toss it, if he hasn't already, and crack open another one. Probably has a glove box full of them." He opened his huge palms toward me. "And life goes on."

"So I guess you're telling me that these people aren't stupid."

"Not by a long shot." He leaned back in his chair and stuffed the four fingers of his right hand beneath his belt. "I just had a chat with Jerry Hyatt, the principal over at the high school. He says that in the past few months he's seen an uptick in kids showing up intoxi-cated or stoned. Not a lot, but some." McCutcheon scratched an ear. "Not sure how he'd notice. I don't think stoned kids are all that uncommon in high schools anymore."

"From what I hear, Hyatt's a hands-on guy," I said. "He takes student issues very seriously. If a trend was to be seen he'd be the guy to see it."

"True. He's definitely hands-on. Unfortunately his hands are also full. I don't see how the guy could do half of what he does and still keep tabs on all his stoned students."

As sad as that was, it was very true. To my mind there were many reasons for it, not the least of which was the ready availability of drugs. Couple that with the fact the classes were usually too big and teachers were overworked and the school system had too little money and the mountain of new rules and regulations and paperwork tied everything in a knot. You mix all that in the blender and you get stoned kids walking the hallways.

Hawkins slipped his glasses off again. "Now you can see why I insisted on us talking face-to-face. I wanted to be sure you understood what we're dealing with."

"I understand completely. Wish I didn't. Wish we didn't have to. Things are very different than when I was in high school."

Hawkins nodded. "And light-years from when I was."

"What can I do?" I asked.

"I want you to help me get the word out. Not just to your doctor friends but to everyone."

"I'll do what I can."

Hawkins smiled. "Don't be so modest. I know about your practice. You see some of the most influential people in the Hamptons. Civic leaders. Community and fund-raising directors. Even the head of the school board if my information is correct."

I shrugged.

"These are the people who can spread the word like a virus in a boot camp. And that's what we need. More eyes and ears. Shut this thing down before something really bad happens."

"I'll call a few of my patients."

"That would help immensely."

"I'll also call the ER director at Hamptons Heritage. He's a good guy, and he stays on top of this kind of stuff. He'll send the word out to all the ERs in the area."

"I've already spoken with Bernard Bernstein over at the Medical Society," Hawkins added. "He's going to send out an e-mail blast to all his members."

Dr. Bernard Bernstein was president of the Suffolk County Medical Society. I had met him before.

McCutcheon massaged his neck. "It's going to be a pain for the department, but let everyone either of you talk to know that we want to be called on any case of amphetamine or ecstasy use that they see or even suspect. I don't know how many the private practitioners and the ER docs see, but I bet it's a lot more than we might think."

The truth is that the police are almost never notified when someone comes to the ER stoned. It's just too common. The police would run themselves ragged taking reports. Most of the stoners that do come in are casual users of things like alcohol and marijuana and occasionally ecstasy and even methamphetamines. Usually confused, disoriented, or with dizziness or vomiting or some other toxic symptom. Unless they've been assaulted or have assaulted someone or been involved in some accident, the police usually aren't called. The user's symptoms are treated and he's sent home. What McCutcheon was telling me was that that was about to change.

Hawkins stood. I did, too. He shook my hand. "Thanks, Hank."

"Thanks for telling me. I know Kevin Moxley's mother will be impressed with what you guys are doing."

"It's for kids like Kevin that this is so important," Hawkins said.

"True." I walked toward the door but stopped and turned back to look at Hawkins and McCutcheon. "I think I'll talk with Principal Hyatt, too. Maybe he has some thoughts on how to combat this."

"I'll let him know to expect your call," McCutcheon said.

I left McCutcheon's office and headed for the high school. On the way I called Divya and told her what I had learned about Kevin Moxley's cute little pink pills.

She was as astonished as I had been. She had just finished the last follow-up and said she'd meet me at the HankMed booth.

"I'll be a few minutes late," I said. "I'm going to swing by and see the principal first."

"It's July. Why would the principal be in his office in July?"

"Because it's a year-round job and because summer school is going on."

"I never thought of that. I just assumed they had a three-month vacation every year."

"Not the principal. Sergeant McCutcheon spoke with him earlier and he said he would be in his office all day, so I thought I'd stop by and talk with him about all this."

"See you shortly."

Here's a life lesson: Never put off anything important. Just do it. If you don't, something equally as important will come along and you'll be behind the curve. Playing catch-up the rest of the day. Doctors know this. That's why they make hospital rounds so early in the morning. Before something big comes along. A sick ER patient. An ICU cardiac arrest. Things that can trash the entire day. Particularly if you're already behind.

To me, calling some of my more influential patients was important and shouldn't be put off. The sooner the word on this new drug got out there, the better. So once I parked in the high school lot, I spent the next thirty minutes calling several of my most well-connected patients. Each was shocked at the story I had to tell and was more than eager to spread the word.

Finally I climbed out of my Saab and set off looking for the principal's office.

That's exactly where I found Jerome Hyatt. I had met him once before and of course knew him by reputation. He had been principal at the high school for more than three decades and was very pro-student. He even demanded that they, and their parents, call him Jerry rather than by his title. That degree of informality could have backfired and led to disrespect, anarchy, and acting out, but Jerry had a knack for garnering respect even in the face of such laxness.

What was truly amazing was that he had kept the job so long, since siding with students meant that he had to butt heads with the board of education on a regular basis. But even the board members seemed to love him, so he survived despite the occasional skirmish.

The outside door to his office was closed but unlocked, so I walked in. His secretary's desk was empty, the computer turned off, so I assumed she was not in today. The interior door that led to his private office was standing open and I saw him, sitting at his desk, head down, reading. I rapped on the doorframe. He looked up.

"Dr. Lawson." He stood and came around the desk to shake my hand. "What a pleasant surprise. Sergeant

McCutcheon called a few minutes ago and said you'd be contacting me." He smiled. "Of course I thought it would be by telephone."

"We're working on our booth for the health fair, so I thought it was easier just to come by and see if you were in."

"Please, have a seat." He retreated to his chair. "This is the time of year that's the hardest. You would think summers would be easy, but with our summer classes as filled as they are and with all the new rules and regulations that are coming into effect next year, like every other year unfortunately, this is what I do with my so-called vacation time." He waved a hand over the stacks of papers on his desk.

"Sounds like the life of a doctor."

"Very true, though maybe not as life-and-death."

"Molding lives is often as important as saving them."

"Perhaps." He shrugged. "But that's not why you're here." He rested his elbows on his desk and laced his fingers before him. "Sergeant McCutcheon told me about this new designer drug." He shook his head. "I just don't understand this."

"I'm not sure I do either, if that's any consolation."

"I'm one of those who won't even take an aspirin. For the life of me I can't understand why anyone would put some unknown and unregulated chemical in their body. It just makes no sense."

"You, of all people, know why," I said. "Teenagers like to live on the edge. Using drugs like this is just part of that."

"Unfortunately that's all too true." He sighed.

I flashed on the old Springsteen song made famous by Manfred Mann. "Blinded by the Light." The lines where Mama told him not to look into the eyes of the sun, to which the reply was that that's where the fun is.

This drug was the eyes of the sun. The users were looking for the fun.

"I understand that this one could be a little more dangerous than the usual," Hyatt said. "Is that how you see it?"

I nodded. "Anytime you start mixing drugs—what we call polypharmacy—things can get sideways. And when you mix two different amphetamines like crystal meth and MDMA, the results can be unpredictable."

His face seemed to collapse, pain written in every crease and a deep sadness in his eyes. Jerry Hyatt loved kids and I was sure that seeing a new destructive force enter their lives made him feel that he had failed them in some way. He of course hadn't, not now and probably not ever, but I knew I would never convince the man sitting before me of that truth, so I didn't try.

Instead I said, "I understand you've noticed an increase in drugs here at school?"

"It's a little soon to tell, but I think so. In the last three months of the school year—say March, April, and May—we sent around a dozen kids home for being in school under the influence of something."

"That's more than usual?"

"Perhaps. It's hard to tell with such a short time span and small sample size. I couldn't say it's a statistically significant difference, but my gut tells me that that many is a slight increase."

"Besides the numbers, was there any difference in the symptoms that the kids displayed?"

He hesitated for a moment, his brow furrowed. "I would say yes. A couple I can remember seemed to be a little more out of it than the typical stoners we see."

"What do you mean by 'out of it'?"

"More erratic behavior. More confused than the typical marijuana user. Maybe even a shade more hostile."

"Did you involve the police in any of those instances?"

"Just once. But that was more about the fight that broke out in the parking lot than about the drugs. Though both of the combatants were obviously intoxicated."

"What's your policy on reporting drug use at school to the police?"

"We try to avoid that if we can. Don't get me wrong—I think drug use is destructive and criminal. But the ramifications of police and court involvement can be equally destructive."

"I can't say I disagree with that."

"Not that I blame the police. It's just that a kid can sometimes become overwhelmed, even consumed, by the system. Take a minor self-limited problem and make it a permanent mark. It's often a tough call."

I nodded. He was right. Same with stoners and tweakers who ended up in the ER. It's a judgment call.

"We almost always talk with the parents," Hyatt continued, "but getting the police involved would probably complicate things and waste their time." He spread his hands flat on the surface of his desk. "These aren't bad kids. They don't really harm anyone. Except themselves, of course. I like to handle these things as a family issue rather than a legal one."

"Unless a fight or something like that is involved?"

"Exactly. Look. Most of them use alcohol, maybe drink a few beers at lunch, and come back in with alcohol on their breath. Some of them sit in their cars and smoke marijuana before coming to class. I've seen that myself." He shrugged. "I don't like it. I do everything I can to fight it. But at the end of the day I'd rather help them, or at least try to, than make a legal issue out of it."

"I understand. And I agree. Most of this is harmless and experimental, and I would assume that most of them will outgrow it and move on with their lives. But I'm worried about this new combination. It has the potential to create some truly bizarre behavior."

"You've made my day," he said with a sad smile. "As if these teenagers didn't have enough going on in their bodies and their brains with all the social and hormonal stuff, now they've got a new drug to throw into the mix." His shoulders slumped and he settled back in his chair.

"I couldn't have said it better."

"I'll keep my eyes and ears open and I'll be a little quicker to call the police than I normally would."

"Let's hope this is a few isolated cases and not the start of something bigger."

"You don't believe that, though, do you?"

"No, I don't. But maybe we can stop it early."

"Let's hope."

Chapter 11

"Point your toes," Danielle said.

"I am. They won't fit through."

"Didn't you try this on at the surf shop?"

"It seemed easier then." Evan struggled to pull on his wet suit, not getting very far. His left foot kept getting stuck, stretching the material. "My foot's too big."

"Bragger."

"What?"

"You know. Big feet—"

"Funny. How come yours just slid right on?"

"My feet are smaller. Besides, I pointed my toes."

"And your suit's much cooler." He flapped one of the arms of his wet suit. "All the cool ones were gone. Something about this being a holiday weekend. So I got stuck with this orange and yellow one."

"It'll be fine."

"But everyone's staring."

"No they're not. Now, let's get you into it and get the lesson started."

Evan sat on the rear bumper of Danielle's SUV and continued his struggles.

"Let me help," she said.

Evan extended his leg toward her. While she tugged and yanked each wet suit leg up over his feet, three teenage boys walked by, snickering and looking at Evan. Their eyes were glassy, pupils wide and black.

"Dude, you trying to get that on or off?" one of them asked.

The other two giggled.

"On."

They burst out laughing.

The apparent leader of the group said, "Why? You'll look like a parrot. A giant yellow and orange parrot."

More giggles.

"A cockatoo," one of the other boys said. "Not a parrot. A cockatoo."

The leader landed a playful punch on the other boy's shoulder. "Dude, you totally slay me."

"Why don't you guys move along?" Danielle said. "Do something useful."

"Uh-oh, his mommy's getting upset."

More laughter as they continued across the parking lot, occasionally glancing back, stumbling as if drunk.

"The youth of America," Danielle said. "And people wonder why we're in trouble."

"They looked stoned to me," Evan said.

"You think? Or it's possible they're just losers."

Danielle gave a final tug and Evan's second foot popped through. "There you go."

Evan rolled the suit up to his waist, leaving the arms dangling at his sides. He looked down at his orange and yellow legs. "I do look like a cockatoo."

"It'll keep you warm. That's the important thing."

"Hank said I'd be shark food in this color."

"I think sharks are color-blind."

"Really?"

"Actually, I don't know, but I thought that'd make you feel better."

"But they do like surfers."

"That's a myth."

"Are you sure? Or are you still trying to make me feel better?"

"Both."

A couple with two small children walked by, heading toward the beach. The man carried a cooler in one hand, his other arm hooked through two beach chairs. The woman had a stack of towels under one arm as she herded the children along. The adults eyed Evan as they walked by.

"People are still staring at me."

"It's your imagination. You look fine."

"Easy for you to say. Your suit's ultracool."

It was. Solid black and form-fitting. Of course it was custom-made for her. One of the perks of being a pro.

"Look at it this way. With that outfit it'll be easy for me to keep track of you in the water," Danielle said.

"Are you sure I need this? It's July."

"The water doesn't know that. You'll be glad you have it when we get out there."

Evan wasn't convinced, since sweat was already collecting beneath the suit.

"It's too crowded here. Let's grab our boards and move down that way." Danielle pointed toward a rock outcropping about a hundred yards away. The beach there had only a few sunbathers.

She pulled open the back door of her SUV, revealing half a dozen surfboards.

"Are all these yours?" Evan asked.

"Yeah."

"Are they expensive?"

"Not for me. My sponsor gives me as many as I want. And wet suits and anything else I need."

"That's so cool," Evan said. "I need a sponsor."

Danielle laughed. "Let's get you up on a board first. Then we'll see about sponsors."

"I'm going to shred it," Evan said.

"Shred it?"

"I read one of those surfer magazines you gave me. Isn't that the current lingo?"

"I think we'll be doing more paddling than shredding today."

"You'll see. Evan R. Lawson is destined to be a great surfer."

Danielle laughed again. "Here, Big Kahuna." She lifted a red-trimmed white board and handed it to him. "This one should work for you."

Evan took it from her and said, "It's not as heavy as it looks."

"Boards are lighter now. Not the old wooden logs of the past." Danielle grabbed her board, ivory with two dark green stripes running its length. "These are my competition boards, so they're very light." She clicked the SUV locks, tucked her board under one arm, and said, "Let's go."

She headed down the beach. Evan followed. Danielle carried her board easily, casually, but Evan struggled with his, not sure exactly how to grip it. He managed, but did drop it a couple of times.

Before they had gone very far, two bathing suit–clad young girls—early teens, Evan guessed—intercepted them. They shielded the sun from their eyes and looked up at Danielle.

"Aren't you Danielle Delaney?" one of them asked.

"Yes. And who are you?"

"I'm Rebecca. This is my friend Alex."

"Nice to meet you."

"We're big fans," Rebecca said. Alex nodded enthusiastically.

"Do you young ladies surf?" Danielle asked.

"No. But we saw that meet you won. On TV. The one in Hawaii."

"The Pipeline meet," Danielle said. "That was a tough one. The waves were fierce."

"Looked that way. I don't know how you stay on the board with all that going on."

"That's the trick, isn't it?"

The girls giggled.

"I can't believe it's really you," Rebecca said. "I can't wait to tell all my friends!"

"I'm flattered."

The two stood awkwardly for a minute.

"Tell you what," Danielle said, nodding toward the camera Rebecca held. "How about a picture together?"

"Really?" the girls said in unison. Their eyes could not have gotten any bigger without exploding.

"Really." Danielle smiled at them.

"That would be so way cool," Rebecca said.

Danielle took the camera and handed it to Evan. "Want to do the honors?"

"My pleasure."

Danielle positioned herself between the girls and Evan took a series of pictures and then handed the camera back to Rebecca.

"There you go," he said.

"Thanks you! Thank you!" Rebecca said.

The girls turned and took off, giggling, with arms waving, toward a group of adults, most likely their parents, who were gathered beneath a pair of umbrellas.

"You just made their day," Evan said. "That was nice of you."

"Fans are one of the things that makes pro surfing fun." She looked at Evan. "And teaching new surfers, of course. Ready?"

"Let's do it."

They continued down the beach. When they cleared the crowd of sunbathers and neared the rocks, Evan headed toward the water.

"Where are you going?" Danielle asked.

"The water. Isn't that where you surf?"

She laughed. "Not yet, Big Kahuna. We start here on the beach."

Evan dragged his board toward her. "Why?"

"Slow down. We'll get in the water soon. First you need to learn a few things."

"Like what?"

"Like how to stand on the board."

"Like this?" Evan dropped the board on the sand and stepped up on it. He wobbled a bit, lost his balance, and one foot slid off onto the sand.

"See?" Danielle laughed. "It's not as easy as it looks."

Evan shrugged. "Okay. What do I do?"

"Lie down on your board." He did. Danielle walked around him. She nudged his foot with her toe. "Move up a little. So you're balanced in the middle."

He wiggled up into position.

"That's it. Now, this is how you'll lie on the board when we head out and when we paddle to catch a wave. Make sure your arms can move freely."

Evan mock-paddled.

"Perfect. Now watch me."

Danielle lay down on her board. "When you catch the wave you'll want to jump up on your knees." She deftly pushed up to a kneeling position. "Make sure you're centered when you do. Now you try it."

"On my knees?" Evan asked. "I thought we were going to stand up."

"Later. You have to crawl before you can walk."

Evan sprang to his knees several times.

"Bet this is easier in the water," Evan said.

"It isn't," Danielle said. "Here the sand balances the board for you. Out there's a different story."

Evan jumped up to his knees and then back down. Then up on his knees again.

"That's it," Danielle said. "Work on that for a few minutes and then we'll try it in the water."

Evan made the move twenty or so times. While he was doing it, he noticed the three teen boys who had harassed him earlier. Up near the edge of the beach, standing next to a van, talking with a couple. The guy was tall and thin, with a ponytail down to the middle of his back; the girl was shorter but also thin and with long, dark hair.

One of the boys exchanged something with the man, both stuffing whatever it was into their pockets. The couple then climbed into the van and drove away while the boys turned back up the beach.

"Looks good," Danielle said. "Let's hit the water."

I found Divya at the HankMed booth.

"How did your meeting with the principal go?"

"He didn't put me in detention, if that's what you mean."

Divya laughed. "That would be more Evan's style."

"True. Jerry Hyatt is as disturbed as we all are over

this new drug. He's going to keep an eye out for it and be a little more proactive about calling in the police."

"Maybe the police can find out where this stuff is coming from and put a stop to it."

"Let's hope. How'd the visits go?"

"Fine. I completed my notes if you want to see them."

"Later."

"I've been thinking about how best to configure the booth," Divya said. "I think the desk is fine there. Maybe an exam table along each side. We'll need some privacy screens, though."

"I'd bet Jill has some we can use."

"Probably. If not, I'll rent them." Divya pointed to the two rear corners. "The portable X-ray can go in one of those corners, and we can stack consumable supplies in the other."

I looked around. "It'll be tight, but we can make it work."

"We can park the van right there, can't we?" She pointed toward the back of the booth. The two rear flaps were tied open, revealing a grassy area.

"I think so. We'll ask Jill."

"That would make things much easier. We can leave some of our equipment in the van that way."

"Maybe keep the X-ray unit in the van until we need it," I said. "That'll open up more space in here."

"Good idea."

I walked to the front of the booth and gazed across at the Hamptons Heritage booth. Several people were working there, but I didn't see Jill among them. "Have you seen Jill?"

"No."

"Let's go find her."

We went out into the middle of the football practice field and turned toward the opposite end, moving along one set of hash marks. The health fair setup was well under way. Each of the goalposts was wrapped in red, white, and blue. Canvas booths completely circled the track that bordered the field. Some sat empty, but others were filled with people prepping for the weekend. A long-jump pit, an obstacle course, a pair of trampolines, a scaffold with three dangling ropes for climbing competitions, and a cluster of gymnastic bars and beams dotted the field itself.

We found Jill near the gymnastics equipment. She gave us a tour, showing us where booths would be for CPR instruction by the American Heart Association, child safety, bicycle safety, skin cancer protection and prevention, home health and safety instruction, smoking cessation and a Tobacco-Free Youth program, drug use intervention and prevention, back health, diabetic testing, hearing testing, eye exams by two local ophthalmologists, nutritional counseling, lung function testing by one of the hospital pulmonologists, and even insurance counseling. There were also commercial booths: Marcy's Bodyworks, Wiggins Waters, Good Vibrations Massage Chairs, Verona's Health Foods and Vitamins, and of course, Fleming's Custom Shop. None of these had been set up yet.

"We're going to have races for the various age groups," Jill said. "Nothing longer than a mile, though. Some relays, too. On Sunday afternoon we'll have Evan's fund-raising walk."

"How are the sign-ups for that going?" Divya asked.

"It's been unbelievable. We have all three hundred slots filled and a waiting list. Thanks to Evan."

"He's obsessed about it for two months," I said.

"His obsession has paid off. He's rounded up folks from various businesses, social clubs, even the PTA and the Chamber of Commerce."

"Maybe that's his true calling," I said. "Maybe he should be a professional fund-raiser."

"Don't forget superspy," Divya said.

"How could I?"

We completed our lap around the field and reached the HankMed booth. Jill pointed across the end zone toward the Hamptons Heritage booth.

"I thought putting the two medical booths near the front and one on each side of the field would be best. That should make them easy to find since everyone will see them as they come in."

"Good idea," I said.

"Of course it is."

"Modest, too."

"I learned it from Evan," Jill said.

"My brother. The king of good ideas."

"Spare me," Divya said.

"A couple of our ER docs will man our booth," Jill said.

"And we'll be here," I said.

"Unfortunately so will superspy Evan R. Lawson," Divya said.

Jill laughed. "You probably won't have to worry with him. Somehow I can't see him hanging around the booth all day. Evan has to schmooze."

"It's what he was born to do," I said.

"What do you think of the space?" Jill asked.

"Love it."

"Besides the desk and the exam tables do you need anything else?"

"Privacy screens," Divya said. "Do you have any of those lying around?"

"I think so. I'll check." She pulled a notepad from her purse and scribbled on it. "I'll add it to the list."

"Don't go out of the way," I said. "We can easily rent them."

"Trust me, it's no problem. We have more stuff in storage than you can imagine. Anything else you can think of right now?"

"Just to be sure," Divya said, "we can park the van right here behind the booth, right?"

"I don't see any reason why not. I know Rachel Fleming will have a couple of her conversions behind her booth."

"That would make things much easier," I said. "We'd have all our equipment and our computers right here."

"Consider it done," Jill said.

"An executive decision? Just like that?"

"Of course. I'm the administrator. I can do what I want."

"Don't let all that power go to your head."

"I thought you said you found strong women sexy."

"There's that, too."

"Should I get a hose?" Divya asked.

Chapter 12

It should be easy. Paddling around on a board that's longer than you are tall. Then kneeling on it and riding a three-foot wave to shore. Piece of cake.

Maybe for most people.

Think Danielle. Most other people, too.

Not so much for others.

Think Evan.

The first two rides had been easy. Those were lying down. Even then Evan wobbled a bit but at least managed to stay on the board. The next three were kneeling. Sort of. Evan fell each time. Zero for three.

To add to Evan's misery, apparently word was out that the great Danielle Delaney was giving a surfing lesson. This drew a couple of dozen people, most standing along the shoreline, others bobbing in the water or floating on Boogie Boards nearby. Most watched quietly, some shouting encouragement, others offering suggestions, and still others simply laughing.

Danielle and Evan lay on their boards, twenty feet apart and a hundred yards offshore, waiting for the next set to build.

"Relax," Danielle said. "Let the wave carry you. Don't fight it."

"I'm not fighting," Evan said. "I'm holding on. It just picks me up and flips me."

"That's because you're trying to make it do what you want it to do instead of just letting it take you with it."

"Like a Slip 'n Slide."

Danielle laughed. "Not exactly, but close."

"Hard to do with an audience."

"Ignore them. Concentrate on what you're doing."

"Come on, dude. You can do it," someone shouted.

"See? You already have a fan."

"One out of twenty."

"That's a start."

They rode up and then down as the first swell of the next set slid beneath them.

Evan now understood the value of a wet suit. The sun was warm but the water cold. Very cold. The bright orange and yellow no longer mattered. Warmth did.

"We'll let the next one go and catch the third," Danielle said. "It'll be the best."

Danielle had earlier explained that every surfer knows about wave sets. They come in two or three up to five or six and sometimes even ten or so with a quiet period in between. Common wisdom says that the third wave in the set is the best, but that's debated. Bottom line? According to Danielle, you take the one that feels right. And if you surf enough, if you've done it since you were a kid, if you're world-class, you usually guess right.

Danielle glanced over her shoulder toward the horizon. "Get ready."

Evan paddled his board into position, nose toward the shore. Danielle did the same, edging closer to Evan.

The next swell lifted him and settled back again.

"Okay, the next one is ours," Danielle said. "When I start paddling you do, too."

"Got it."

"When you get going, jump up to your knees. Just like you were doing on the beach."

"Seemed easier there."

"Let's go."

Danielle began stroking the water; Evan followed. Danielle jumped to her feet, Evan to his knees. He rode that way for maybe twenty yards and then collapsed to his left. The wave churned over him, spinning him for a couple of loops. He felt the board tug at the leash attached to his ankle. Finally the wave spit him out. He came up gasping, at first treading water, but then his feet discovered the bottom, so he stood. He corralled his board.

Danielle stood closer to shore in waist-deep water watching him. "You okay?" she asked.

"Fine." He swiped water from his face with the palm of one hand.

"Actually, that was much better. You got up and rode the wave."

"Not very far."

"Still, you rode it. Now let's go do it again. I bet next time you'll finish the ride."

They paddled back out and loitered for a few minutes, waiting for the next set. The gentle rise and fall of the ocean relaxed Evan. He looked up and down the beach, now packed with sunbathers, umbrella-shaded families and couples, and kids of all ages splashing around. He had never really felt comfortable in the water, but sitting here on a surfboard next to Danielle was pretty cool.

"This is great," Evan said. "I can see why you do it."

"It'll be even better when you learn a little more."

"You mean when I can actually stand up."

"That's right. But we'll save that for another day. Right now I want you to master riding on your knees."

"I've got it," Evan said. "This time all the way to shore."

"That's the spirit." Danielle glanced back. "Here comes number one. When the third one arrives I want you to paddle extra hard. Get out in front of it."

Evan did. The wave caught his board and jerked him forward. He snapped up to his knees. He rode the wave, this one slightly bigger than the last. He caught Danielle from the corner of his eye. She was standing, cutting her board back and forth to stay near him.

It was perfect.

He was actually doing it.

It felt easy and he relaxed, letting the wave carry him.

Then it happened.

He leaned too far to the right. His board followed. He and Danielle collided in a twisting mass of arms and legs and flying boards.

Evan struck the bottom. Air surged out of his lungs. The water seemed to pick him up and spin him in every direction. He felt dizzy. Up and down seemed the same. Right and left, too. Then his knees dragged along the coarse sand. The spinning stopped and he finally managed to get his feet planted and stood up in waist-deep water. His board smacked against his back, knocking him off balance. He quickly regained his footing and looked toward shore, where a group of people stood, wide-eyed, some with hand to mouth, some looking past him and pointing.

He turned, thinking for sure a shark would be bearing down on him. A big shark. Like the one in *Jaws*. Big enough to eat a boat. Big enough to swallow him whole. He'd known the orange and yellow wet suit was a bad idea.

But there was no shark. Instead he saw Danielle standing chest-deep in the water, clutching her right shoulder and grimacing.

"Are you okay?" Evan asked.

"I don't think so."

"Your shoulder?"

She nodded. "I felt it pop." She tried to move it but winced. "Let's get out of the water."

"I'll call Hank. He'll know what to do."

"How about here?" I asked.

"A little," Danielle said.

She was sitting in a chair on our Shadow Pond patio, wearing cutoff jeans and a tank top. I stood next to her, examining her shoulder. I pressed another area and she winced and recoiled.

"That's it," she said.

I nodded.

"What is it?"

"Probably an AC separation."

She shook her head. "That's what I was afraid of." She took a deep breath and let it out slowly. "I had a friend with this once. A big wave rider. Hit the bottom out at Mavericks. Near San Francisco. Took him four months to recover." She looked up at me. "Is that what I'm looking at?"

I shrugged. "Maybe."

"Great. I have a big meet in six weeks. Down in South Africa."

"I'm sorry," Evan said. "I don't know what happened."

"You knocked me off my board," Danielle said.

Evan was frantic. He walked around waving his arms. "I know." He stopped next to Danielle and looked at her. "I didn't mean to."

"It's okay," she said. "I'm just pimping you. These things happen."

"What can I do? I mean . . . what can I do?"

"Nothing. It'll heal. And missing a meet isn't the end of the world." She laughed. "My sponsors might see it differently, but they'll just have to deal with it."

"Before we write everything off," I said, "let me get an X-ray and see how severe it is."

"That'll tell you?" Danielle asked.

"Sure will."

"Maybe it's not so bad," Evan said.

"Want to help me find out?" I asked.

"How?"

"Go get the X-ray machine from the van."

Twenty minutes later Divya and I had completed the X-rays and loaded the data on my laptop. I sat at the kitchen table, Danielle next to me, Evan and Divya huddled behind us. I scrolled through the images, carefully examining each one, before returning to the one that best showed the problem.

"This is the clavicle, the collarbone." I pointed to it with my pen. "This is the scapula or shoulder blade. This projection off the scapula is called the acromion. Okay?"

"Yeah," Danielle said.

"Right here where they join is called the acromioclavicular joint. The AC joint."

"That's the sore spot on top of my shoulder?" Danielle asked.

"That's it. See this gap here?" She nodded. "It should be a little narrower."

"That's the separation?"

"Sure is. The good news is that yours is minor. More a ligament strain than a true separation."

"So it's not too bad?" Evan asked.

"I've seen worse. Much worse. A severe separation can require surgery." I turned and looked at Danielle. "Which would put you out of action for months." She frowned. "But this? It'll be sore for a few weeks, but it'll heal."

"No surgery?"

"A couple of days in a sling with ice packs and then rehab exercises and you'll be fine."

"Will I miss the South Africa meet?"

"Depends on how fast you heal. But it will definitely cut into your training."

"I can deal with that, but I'd hate to miss the trip."

"Let's see how things progress over the next ten days," I said. "Will you still be here?"

"I plan to be."

"Then we'll keep an eye on it."

She nodded. "Sounds good."

"I would suggest you not get back in the water with Evan," Divya said.

"It was an accident," Evan said. "It could have happened to anyone."

Divya crossed her arms, cocking her head to one side. "Even a superspy?"

Danielle laughed. "Okay, guys, let's not pick on Evan too much. It was partly my fault. I stayed too close to him. Should've kept more distance."

"We are all trying to discover how to do that," Divya said.

Danielle stood. "I need to get home and start dinner for Grandma."

"Can I help?" Evan asked.

"She's still healing from her last injury," Divya said. "I'm not sure she could handle another one."

"It was an accident."

"She's teasing you," Danielle said. "Why don't you come over tonight? I'm making fish tacos, and we have plenty. Grandma would love it."

"Okay. That would be fun. What time?"

"Maybe seven?"

"Cool."

Chapter 13

By evening a drizzle had set in, followed by a healthy rain, which thankfully lightened by the time Evan pulled to a stop in Angela Delaney's gravel parking area. The sun was low and the water-soaked trees cast long shadows over the house. Rain circles and a few bubbles dotted the surface of the pond.

Evan jumped from his car and dodged a few water-filled potholes as he scurried for the cover of the rear porch. He had a bottle of wine in one hand and an empty plastic document binder in the other, holding it over his head as a quasi umbrella. He had forgotten to bring a real one.

As he climbed the porch steps, the rear door swung open. Danielle held it with her good arm. The other arm was in a sling.

"Love your umbrella," she said.

"It's the best I could come up with." He flapped it a couple of times, shaking off the water. "At least it's slowed down some." He placed the plastic cover on the table that sat between Angela's porch rockers. "I'll leave it here. I might need it when I leave."

Danielle led him into the living room, where Angela sat in a wingback chair, her leg propped on an ottoman. She closed the book she held and placed it next to the lamp on the table to her left.

"Look who the rain drove in," Angela said. "Did you get wet, dear?"

"Not much."

"Have a seat," Angela said. "Danielle will get you something to drink."

"I brought wine." He held up the bottle. "White." He looked at Danielle. "You are making fish tacos, right?"

"Yes." She reached for the bottle. "I'll open it."

"Maybe I should," Evan said. "It might be hard to do with one hand."

"You're probably right. Come on."

She led him into the kitchen. It was small but looked as if it belonged in an architectural magazine. Pale yellow walls, multipaned white-trimmed windows, dark yellow tieback curtains, ceramic tile countertops, natural wood cabinets, and a freestanding square chopping block in the middle of the floor.

"We're also having rice, corn, and black beans." She indicated three pots on the stovetop. She retrieved a wine opener from a drawer and handed it to him. "Now that you're here I'll put the fish in." She pulled open the oven, lifted a baking pan filled with glistening white fillets, and slid it onto the rack. All with one hand.

"You're pretty good for only being able to use one arm."

"And whose fault might that be?"

"I told you, it was . . ."

She interrupted him by snapping a dish towel at him. "I'm teasing you."

"I know, but I still feel guilty." The wine cork popped free.

"Good." She laughed. "The fish will only take a few minutes and then we'll be ready for dinner."

"I'm starving."

"Surfing will do that to you." She took three wine-glasses from an overhead cabinet and placed them on the chopping block.

"I'm not sure what I did would qualify as surfing."

"You worked hard."

"Too hard." He began to fill the glasses. "How's your shoulder doing?"

"Beginning to get stiff and sore."

"I'm so sorry."

"No more about that. I told you, stuff happens." She picked up one of the wineglasses. "This will help." She took a sip. "Very good."

"Anything I can do to help?"

"Go entertain Grandma. It'll be ready in a few minutes."

Evan took a glass of wine to Angela and sat on the sofa.

"How are you doing?" he asked.

"Better than Danielle." She flashed a devilish grin.

"It was an accident."

"I'm teasing you."

"Do you two have the same writer?"

Angela laughed. "Don't need one. She's basically my clone. Always has been." She sighed. "I see so much of myself in her."

"Well, that's a good thing."

"Yes, it is." She lifted her wineglass toward him and then took a sip. "My, this is good."

"The man at the wine store suggested it."

"He did a good job." She took another sip. "Truth is that Danielle has always suffered bumps and bruises. A real tomboy like I was. From tree climbing as a child to all types of sports. Seemed she was always doing something to something."

"This wasn't her fault. It was mine."

"She'll heal. She always does."

"But she might miss that meet in South Africa."

"Bet she doesn't."

"Bet she doesn't what?" Danielle said as she entered the living room.

"Miss your next meet, dear."

Danielle moved her shoulder slightly. "I don't know. This is getting pretty sore."

Angela laughed. "If I had a nickel for every time I've heard you say that."

Danielle gave a one-shouldered shrug.

"She would always say that and then the next day go out and wax the competition."

Danielle rolled her eyes. "Don't listen to anything she says."

"Why, dear? It's all true."

"Five minutes." Danielle looked at Evan. "Why don't you help Grandma to the dining table and I'll bring everything out?"

"I can get myself there," Angela said. "You go help Danielle." She swung her leg off the ottoman and stood. "See?"

"I'll take your wine," Evan said.

"That would help."

The dinner was perfect. The beans, the rice, the corn, and especially the broiled fish splashed with fresh-squeezed lime juice and rolled in corn tortillas. Evan devoured four of the tacos.

While they ate, they talked about Danielle's career, HankMed and Evan's work, and of course Danielle's childhood. Angela told an unending series of stories that drew laughter from Evan and a red face and the occasional "Grandma, don't tell that" from Danielle. Angela always waved her away and went on with the story.

While they finished up a dessert of raspberry sherbet, the conversation turned to Angela's rehab. She was frustrated with her slow progress, but Danielle said she was simply expecting too much too soon.

"The PT techs said you were doing well and were ahead of schedule," Danielle said.

"Doesn't feel that way to me. Feels like I'm an invalid. Confined to my house."

"Your surgeon said you could go out. In fact, he insisted, didn't he?"

Angela rolled her eyes. "He's not old."

Evan laughed. "Neither are you."

"Are you blind? Look at me."

"You're beautiful."

Angela raised an eyebrow to Danielle. "I told you he was a charmer."

"But he's right. You are beautiful—and you need to get out of the house."

"I tell you what," Evan said. "Tomorrow morning I'll buy breakfast. There's a great place over in East Hampton. You'll love it."

"That would be great," Danielle said. "And then maybe we'll go shopping or something."

"You two go. I'll stay here."

"No." Evan and Danielle said in unison.

"But what if I fall or something?"

"I'll be there," Danielle said.

"And I'll bring Hank and Divya."

Angela nodded and then a smile appeared. "That would be nice." She folded her napkin and laid it on the table. "Okay, it's a date."

Chapter 14

Yesterday's rain had scrubbed the air, leaving the morning sky bright blue and cloudless. I decided to drive my trusty Saab down to the beach for a run. Several other people apparently had the same idea, and the beach road, two lanes that paralleled the beach, was crowded with joggers, walkers, and bicyclists.

As I ran I considered how far HankMed had come. I remembered when it first started. When Evan came up with the name. When Divya hired herself as my physician assistant. When we had no patients, except for Boris and the young lady who had fallen ill at his party, and to my mind no chances of attracting anyone to the practice. We had only my stethoscope, the trunk full of equipment that Divya had brought with her, and Evan's irrepressible nature.

My, how things had changed. Not Evan's nature—that wasn't going to happen—but just about everything else.

The practice was now booming. We had an ever-increasing population of patients, both mansion dwellers and normal folks who lived in modest houses and still worked for a living. Our clientele reached from Westhampton to Sag Harbor to East Hampton and we even had a few that came out from the city. Of course they came to their weekend homes, but they tended to hold off any doctor visits until they were here.

The HankMed van was a huge success and greatly helped the practice. That was all Evan's doing. Left to my own devices, I could never have made it happen. Fortunately, Evan got the idea in his head and wouldn't let go until the van was secured.

My brother the bulldog.

I have to admit that it was a brilliant idea. I've even told him that a couple of times. When I can tolerate his preening and prancing, that is.

By the time I finished my run and showered, Evan was up and Divya had arrived at Shadow Pond. The three of us restocked the van and then headed into downtown East Hampton to meet Danielle and Angela for breakfast at Frankie's Café. It was Angela's first venture out of her house since her surgery.

Last night when Evan told me about his breakfast plans, he said that Angela was apprehensive about leaving her house and that she'd feel better if Divya and I came along. I agreed immediately and convincing Divya to come took no time.

Most patients who have undergone a hip replacement go through the same anxiety when first getting back into the world and away from the protective environment of the hospital or home. This type of surgery leaves you feeling fragile and makes you walk with great care for fear of falling or stumbling and damaging the new body part. After a few ventures into the world these fears evaporate and life goes on, but the first one can seem daunting.

We parked in the lot half a block off Main Street and walked back to Frankie's. A white-and-green-striped awning shaded the wall of windows that fronted the sidewalk. The place was packed, but I saw that Danielle and Angela had snagged a table near the windows. Danielle waved to us.

"Have you been waiting long?" I asked.

"Just a couple of minutes."

As soon as we settled at the table, a waitress appeared.

"Good morning," she said. "I'm Sandy. Can I get you guys some coffee or tea?"

Everyone ordered coffee. She returned with a fresh pot and filled the five cups and then handed each of us a menu. "I'll be back in a couple minutes to take your order."

"How are you doing?" I asked Angela.

"I'm fine. I wish everyone would quit fussing over me."

"He's not fussing," Danielle said. "He's your doctor and he's simply asking how you're doing."

"I'm fine. Just a little out of sorts and more than a little frustrated."

"And your anxieties about getting back into the world are common," I said. "Everyone goes through it."

"I know. I just want to be my old self again."

"You will," I said. "I know this can all be frustrating. Someone as active as you being slowed down like this is never fun."

"And don't forget that walker. How did I get to be such an old lady all of a sudden?"

"That's not true," I said. "You're much younger than most people your age."

"Thank goodness. I thought you were going to say I was no lady." She gave me a mischievous grin.

I held up my hands. "You'll never hear that from me."

"Even if it's true," Danielle said. She wrapped an arm around Angela's shoulders. "You're no lady, Grandma. You're a broad. One of the all-time-great broads."

Angela laughed. "It's true. Your grandfather used to say that all the time."

"What are you guys up to today?" I asked.

"I think Grandma and I will do a little shopping. Get her back into the world."

"Good idea," I said. "Just don't wear yourself out."

"Won't take long," Angela said. "I need to get back into shopping shape."

"And then while Grandma takes her nap, maybe I'll run over to the costume shop." She looked at Evan. "Are we still doing that?"

I looked at Evan and then Danielle.

"Evan invited me to the big costume party."

The waitress reappeared and took our orders. I

chose oatmeal and fruit while everyone else had eggs and bacon. Sandy said she would have it out in a few minutes

"So you're going to be a spy, too?" Divya asked.

"Unless we consider another option," Evan said.

Divya crossed her arms and leaned back in her chair. "Don't tell me you've finally decided to go as a book-keeper."

"Bookkeeper?" Danielle asked.

"Ignore her," Evan said. "She likes to make jokes."

"Some targets are simply too inviting."

Danielle laughed. "Last night, after Evan invited me, he said he was going as a spy. I thought that would be cool, but then he said that Hank and—Jill, is it?"

"That's right," I said.

"He said you guys were at first going as highway-men but changed your minds."

"That's true."

"So Evan said that we might do that. Go as high-waymen."

"Like a pair of thieves?" Divya asked.

Evan nodded. "Wouldn't that be cool?"

"It's basically the same outfit," I said. "Boots, hat, and a cape."

"Maybe you could throw in an eye patch," Divya said. "That might make you look more sinister."

"And then of course you'd have to have a pistol stuffed down your pants," I said. "No self-respecting bandit would be found without his gun."

"Evan with a gun in his pants would be dangerous,"

Divya said. "He might shoot himself in a very indelicate location."

Danielle laughed. "Actually he's not so much concerned about that as he is about giving up the cane he's been working on."

I looked at him over the cup of coffee I held. "What cane might that be?"

"A spy cane," Evan said. "One with a secret knife and a secret compartment for keeping poisons and messages."

"In your hands that could be almost as dangerous as a gun," Divya said.

"Stick with the spy," I said. "It suits you."

Evan held up his cell phone.

Evan R Lawson is a superspy.

After we left the restaurant, Evan caught a ride with Danielle and Angela, saying he needed to swing by Shadow Pond and pick up his car. He had a meeting scheduled with the manager of a new restaurant who was looking for someone to handle his employee health care program.

"What restaurant?" Divya asked.

"Renée's Bistro. It opened a few weeks ago. Down at the beach."

"I saw it," Danielle said. "It's near where we surfed."

"Surfing?" Divya said. "Is that what it was?"

Danielle laughed. Evan scowled but didn't engage. I was surprised, since restraint wasn't one of his strongest qualities.

"They have a dozen full-time and twice as many part-time employees," Evan said. "And they have no one doing their medical stuff. And best of all they've already agreed to hire HankMed, so today all I have to do is get the contract signed."

"Good job," I said.

"I agree," Divya said.

Evan pulled his cell out. "Would you say . . ."

"Absolutely not," Divya snapped.

After Evan, Danielle, and Angela drove away, Divya and I climbed into the HankMed van. First stop: the Bagel Shack to pick up coffee and an egg, ham, and cheese bagel sandwich before heading over to see Jill. I would have gotten her something at Frankie's, but she loved Bagel Shack. Especially their coffee.

When we reached the high school, nearly a hundred cars, trucks, and even a couple of motor homes were in the parking lot. The setup for the health fair was now in full swing. We continued through the two wide-open chain-link entry gates to the field area, veered to the left, and parked directly behind the evolving HankMed booth.

We locked the van and set out in search of Jill.

There were people everywhere, busily at work organizing their booths and preparing for the various athletic events. Right across the field from the HankMed booth several hospital employees were working on the extra-large Hamptons Heritage booth. We walked over. Jill wasn't there. One of the nurses, who was stocking a cabinet with medical supplies, said she might be at the obstacle course. Last she'd heard, she was headed that way.

That's where we found her—in the middle of the obstacle course that was being set up in one half of the football field. She stood at the end of the chalked long-jump runway watching two workers smooth the sand in the rectangular landing area with rakes. One of the obstacles the kids would have to negotiate. Just beyond it, another worker held a hose and was filling an equally long plastic tub, transforming it into a one-foot-deep water hazard. Beyond that, a series of two-foot-high bars to jump and finally a six-foot wall with a dangling rope to scale. I suspected that by sunset tomorrow there would be some very tired, wet, and sandy kids for exhausted parents to deal with.

Jill saw us coming and reached for the coffee before I had a chance to offer it to her.

"Man, I need this," she said.

"Somehow I figured that would be the case."

Divya held up the bag. "We also brought breakfast."

"You guys are geniuses. All I've had today is coffee, and I'm starving."

I looked around. "Where do you want to sit?"

"Let's walk over to your booth." She headed that way and we followed. "Have you begun stocking it yet?"

"No. We have the supplies we'll need in the van. But I suspected I'd better get you your coffee and some food before dallying there."

She laughed. "You're a lot smarter than you look."

"Don't bite the hand that feeds you."

"Divya has the food, so I think I'm safe there."

"The abuse I have to put up with."

"Poor baby. Divya, can you hear the violins playing?"

"Constantly."

"You guys should have your own TV show."

We reached the HankMed booth. When we'd walked by earlier, I hadn't noticed the three aluminum-framed, green cloth privacy screens that now stood against one wall.

I examined them. "You find these in storage?"

"In the basement. We have more if you need them."

"This should do. Thanks."

"You have two extension cords," Jill said, pointing toward the pair of bright orange electrical cables coiled in one corner. "With two multi-plug outlets. If you think you might need more, I can make that happen."

"I think this'll be fine," I said. "Unless Divya thinks differently."

Divya shook her head. "The computer will be on the desk and plug in there. The ultrasound machine, the digital microscope, and the portable X-ray, if we need them, there. This should work well."

Jill snatched the bagel from the bag, peeled off the wrapper, and took a bite. "Mmm. This is wonderful."

Divya sat behind the desk, and Jill and I each took an exam table, facing each other, feet dangling.

"Looks like it's going to be a great weekend," I said. "We heard the weather report on the way over—it's supposed to be mid-eighties and sunny all the way through the middle of next week."

"When it started raining yesterday, I thought, 'Oh great, it's going to rain all weekend,'" Jill said.

"The eternal optimist."

Jill took a sip of her coffee. "Are you trying to say I worry too much?"

"Not at all."

"Right. Anyway, I would hate for rain to mess up all the stuff we've planned. The kids would be disappointed."

"If the weather report is right," I said, "you have nothing to worry about."

"The operative phrase there is 'if the weather report is right,'" Divya said. "Seems to me they're about fifty-fifty."

"At best," I said.

"Excuse me."

The voice came from just outside the booth. I looked up to see a woman standing there with a young girl. The girl had a bloodstained white towel pressed to her forehead.

"Are you Dr. Lawson?" the woman asked.

"That's right."

"Would you mind taking a look at my daughter? I know you're not set up yet, but I'm not sure what else to do. Except take her to the hospital."

"What happened?" I asked, indicating the towel.

"She banged her head on the edge of the car door."

"Stupid, huh?" the girl said.

"Not really. And not an uncommon injury." I jumped off the exam table and patted its vinyl surface. "Hop up here and I'll take a look."

The contract signed, Evan stood at the edge of the shared parking lot that extended between the newly minted Renée's Bistro and a seafood restaurant that had been there for more years than anyone could remember. Three teenage boys walked by, each in baggy trunks, no shoes, no shirts. Evan recognized them as the kids he had seen at the beach the other day. The ones that had harassed him about his wet suit. They didn't seem to recognize him, however.

"I don't see them," one of the boys said.

"Chill, dude," another one said. "They'll be here."

Evan watched them as they continued toward the far end of the lot and then returned his gaze to the flat, peaceful ocean. He recalled sitting out there with Danielle, gently rocking on the waves. He remembered the thrill of actually riding the board. The speed he reached, even on the face of a small wave, was amazing. He couldn't imagine riding the kinds of waves Danielle surfed. He had seen them on TV, but now he had a new appreciation for what surfers actually did.

Riding that one wave would have made the day perfect had he not crashed into Danielle. It was still way cool.

As he turned toward his car he saw the three boys standing beside the black van he had seen before, talking with the same stringy-haired couple. The girl and one of the boys exchanged something. Evan couldn't tell what from where he stood, but he had a pretty good idea. She stuffed something into the back pocket of her jeans as the boys turned and walked away.

Evan climbed into his car and drove toward them. By the time he reached the van, the boys were gone. He pulled up next to the couple.

"What are you doing?" Evan asked.

"None of your business," the guy said.

He and the girl climbed into the van and drove away. Only after they had left the lot and melted into traffic did Evan realize he should have gotten their license plate number. How stupid. How unspylike.

Evan R. Lawson, superspy, suddenly didn't feel so superspyish.

Chapter 15

After I repaired the young lady's minor forehead laceration and sent her and her mom on their way, with a promise that either Divya or I would stop by their home to remove the stitches in five days, Jill, Divya, and I discussed how best to set up our booth. This was going well until my cell phone rang. It was Evan. He was having wardrobe issues. Something about his spy cape not looking right or not fitting right or not creating the proper image. I could barely hear him as his voice came and went. I knew he had me on speakerphone and I pictured him flitting around the room as he talked. I finally managed to get a few words in and told him that his costume issues weren't a high priority right now.

"But if this doesn't work I have to decide on something else." He had now picked up his cell phone and his voice was clearer.

"Evan, we're a bit busy. I'm sure you can figure out your costume."

"Costume?" Jill asked.

Evan obviously heard her. "Is that Jill? Let me talk to her. She'll know what to do."

I punched the speakerphone button on my cell. "Evan's having problems with his costume and wants to ask your advice."

"I thought his costume was all settled," Jill said.

I shrugged. "You know Evan."

"What's that supposed to mean?" Evan asked.

"That you're a royal pain."

"What's the problem?" Jill asked.

Evan went on about how this didn't fit or that didn't look right or this other thing looked silly. Both Jill and I tried to settle him down, but it was a war of attrition and Evan usually won those. I finally said that Jill was busy, but Divya and I would come by as soon as we could. Then I closed my phone and slipped it back into my pocket.

"Sounds like a house call," Jill said with a laugh. "Or should I say 'home call'?"

"More like a psychotherapy visit."

"Better you than me."

"Unfortunately," Divya said, "I get dragged into it, too."

"Guilt by association," Jill said.

"Or maybe collateral damage," I offered.

"Let's go," Divya said. "The sooner we deal with this the sooner we can get our work done."

Divya and I began repacking the medical bag.

"Are we still on for dinner tonight?" Jill asked me.

"Sure."

"What time?"

"Around six thirty." I looked at Divya. "Join us. We're going to that new Italian place."

"No. I don't want to intrude."

"Intrude?" Jill asked. "You could never do that. Please come."

Divya hesitated a beat and then said, "Okay. I'll meet you there."

"Are you going to pick me up or should I meet you at your place?" Jill asked.

"Either way is fine with me."

Jill hooked her arm in mine. "Picking me up might seem too much like a real date."

"It is a real date."

"Are you getting me flowers?"

"Now you're pushing it."

"Then it's not a real date. I'll be at your place at six."

"You sure?"

"I'm sure." She gave me a playful slap on the backside. "Go help Evan. I have a lot to do here and I better get to it if I'm going be ready on time."

"Are you sure we shouldn't stay around and help?"

"I can handle it. Don't worry."

"Are you saying I'm in the way?"

"Let's say you're distracting."

"Hmm. I like the sound of that."

Jill rolled her eyes. "Divya, get him out of here."

Divya grabbed my arm and pulled me toward the van. "Let's go get Evan's therapy session done," she said. "The longer we wait, the worse it'll be."

True. Evan could whip himself into a frenzy over anything. Even a costume.

Before going to Shadow Pond and dealing with Evan's imaginary emergency, we swung by Kevin Moxley's house. I know we were taking a risk by letting Evan stew a bit longer, but I wanted to see Kevin first. With any luck Evan would exhaust himself before we got there and be easier to handle. Sometimes procrastination is a good thing. Hopefully this would be one of those times.

Rosemary Moxley beamed when she opened the door.

"Dr. Lawson, Divya. I'm so glad you came by."

"Is everything okay?" I asked.

"Absolutely." She was over-the-top happy. Almost giddy. "Please come in."

"And Kevin?" I asked. "He's okay?"

"Never better. Thanks to you and those two police officers."

She led us into the living room and sat down on the sofa, while Divya and I took the two flanking chairs.

"It's like the light in his eyes flipped back on," Rosemary continued. "I think your little photo montage—he showed it to me—got his attention. Then Sergeant Mc-Cutcheon scared him half to death."

"Sometimes that's what teenagers need," Divya said.

"Well, it worked for Kevin. He apologized for everything and swore he would never do that stuff, or anything else, ever again. He cleaned his room, did all the dishes, and even swept the pool deck. Without me asking him to."

"That's great," I said.

"He's talking about getting back into sports as soon as school starts. He even called his coaches and apologized to them."

"Is he here?"

"In his room. I'll get him."

I stood. "Let me go talk with him."

"Sure." She looked at Divya. "I'm sorry. I'm so wrapped up in Kevin I forgot to offer you anything to drink."

"Not necessary," Divya said.

"I just made some fresh coffee."

"Okay."

I left Divya and Rosemary and walked down the hallway to Kevin's room. The door stood open, a good sign, meaning he didn't have secrets to keep. Kevin sat at his desk, his back to me, hunched over an open book. I rapped a knuckle on the doorframe.

"Kevin?"

He turned. "Dr. Lawson."

"Your mom tells me you've decided school and sports are back on your radar."

He nodded his head. "I can't believe how stupid I was."

I sat on the bed next to his chair. I saw that the book

he had been studying was an algebra text. "How did you come to that conclusion?"

"Look." He waved a hand around the room. "I have a great room. My own computer. A great mom. I go to one of the best schools."

"All true."

"And I thought about all the stoners I go to school with. They're brain-dead losers. I don't want to be that dude. I miss my friends and I miss sports. School, too."

"And the algebra book? Getting a head start on next year?"

"I wish. Trying to catch up on all the stuff I should've learned last year."

"You're making smart choices, Kevin. That'll pay off in the long run. And I know your mom is thrilled."

He nodded. "Thank you. The pictures you showed me were freaky. I scouted out some more. On the Internet. That stuff will mess you up."

Yes, it will. And that's not the half of it.

When I returned to the living room, I saw that Rosemary's eyes were red and glassy with tears.

"What's the matter?" I asked.

"Nothing now," Rosemary said. "But I was losing him. You talked some sense into him."

"I merely showed him where he was headed if he didn't take control. I think it scared him."

She dabbed at her eyes with a crumpled napkin. "He's a good boy."

"Yes, he is. And he'll be fine, I think."

*　　*　　*

"It doesn't look right," Evan said.

Evan was in full wardrobe panic. On the basis of his earlier phone call and what I could see before me, he was having issues with the cape that came with his colonial spy outfit. He kept spinning, the chocolate brown cape flaring around him.

"It looks just fine," Divya said. "Quit spinning around before you knock something off the table." She crossed her arms. "Tell him," she said to me.

"Tell him what?" I said. "That he's an idiot?"

"That, too. But tell him that the cape is just fine."

"Looks okay to me."

Evan did a complete three-sixty and as he did he overturned a candle that sat on the coffee table. Fortunately it wasn't lit.

Divya walked over and righted it. "I told you not to do that."

"Perhaps you could exchange it for a red one," I said. "Then you could go as Little Red Riding Hood."

"Funny," Evan said.

Divya laughed. "Maybe a powder blue one with a shepherd's crook and you could be Little Bo Peep."

"Still not funny. But look, I do have this cool cane." Evan picked up a black cane with a faux crystal knob on the end. He began to twist the crystal and soon it came off. "It has a secret compartment here for hiding messages."

"Perhaps cyanide might be more appropriate," Divya said.

Evan ignored her and went on about the cane. About

how he could hide a weapon in the point. Maybe one that retracted like a switchblade. Or maybe even a spring-loaded dart gun. Or maybe even a real gun. He was wound up now.

"You do know this is just a costume?" I asked.

"Still, a knife blade or something would be cool."

"Did you say 'fool'?" Divya said.

"I think maybe just walking around with it will be cool enough," I said. "I wouldn't want you doing any harm to yourself. Or anyone else."

Divya's brow furrowed as she circled Evan, examining his outfit. "Come to think of it, you look a bit like a magician." She snapped her fingers. "I have it. You could be the Great Evandini."

"And make things disappear," I said. "Like yourself."

Evan walked to the wall mirror near the entrance door and did a couple of turns. "It could be a magician's cape."

"Evan was big into magic as a kid," I said.

"Really?" Divya asked.

"You bet," Evan said, spinning toward her. "Dad bought me this kit. I could do card tricks, make rubber balls disappear and reappear, and even do that stuff with the scarves up your sleeve."

"It's true," I said. "He actually got quite good at it. For a while anyway."

"There's a story there."

"No, there isn't," Evan said.

"Actually there is. Evan wanted a rabbit and a top hat. He got the hat but not the rabbit. So he pouted for a while and . . ."

"I didn't pout."

"And you never got a rabbit either."

"Poor Evan." Divya's lower lip drooped in an exaggerated pout.

"So he gave up magic," I said.

"You can't be a good magician without a rabbit," Evan said.

"Sure you can," Divya said. "You can pull other things out of a hat."

"And don't forget making stuff disappear," I said.

Evan spread the cape wide with one hand and with the other raised the cane high, tilting it back and forth as he waved it over Divya's head. "Begone."

Divya stood there staring at him. He stared back, as if he was surprised that she actually hadn't disappeared in a puff of smoke. Sometimes my brother believes his own shtick.

"Maybe you should stick with the scarf tricks," Divya said.

"Or you could be my assistant and I could saw you in half."

"Perhaps not."

I could see the wheels turning in Evan's head. I wasn't sure where they were going, but I suspected he was envisioning himself doing exactly that.

"Did they have magicians back then?" Evan asked.

"Magicians and sorcerers have been around for thousands of years," I said. "But I think being a spy would be best."

Evan grabbed the front of the cape and furled it around himself. "And we all know that I am Evan R. Lawson, superspy."

"As much as I am enjoying this conversation, I have work to do," Divya said.

She sat at the table, pulled her laptop from her bag, and popped it open. While it booted up she extracted a stack of patient notes.

I sat down across from her and opened my laptop. Divya was already busy updating files and Evan continued to spin in his cape. I began to work and after a few minutes noticed that Evan was no longer there.

"Where'd he go?" I asked Divya.

"Probably to find a mirror." She never looked up from her work. "Don't worry. He'll be back."

She was right. Evan came back into the dining room. Cape-less and cane-less.

"Did you get bored with your costume?" Divya asked.

"No. But you're probably right. This outfit is fine as it is."

Was this my brother talking?

My cell phone rang.

It was the radiology department at Hamptons Heritage with a report on Felicia Hecht's MRI. I listened to the verbal report and then asked them to e-mail it to me. I then called the cardiology department and learned that Dr. Walter Edelman, one of the cardiologists on staff, had just finished reading her Holter monitor. The secretary said she didn't yet have the report but that Dr. Edelman was still in the department reading EKGs if I wanted to talk with him. I did. He told me what he had seen on Felicia's Holter and said he would send a complete report once it was typed up. I thanked him and hung up.

"Want to go see Felicia Hecht with me?" I asked Divya.

"Sure. What did you find out?"

"I'll tell you on the way."

"I'll drive," Evan said.

"As long as we don't have to discuss costuming any further," Divya said.

Divya and I found Felicia Hecht in her garden. Exactly where she'd said she would be when I called to tell her we were coming over. She said she had a dozen shrubs to get in the ground, so we should come around to the back when we arrived.

She was bent over a hole in the ground settling the root-ball of a shrub in place. She then dropped to her knees, scooped handfuls of dirt into the hole, and patted it down firmly. Her hair was tied into a wad at the back of her head, except for one strand that had escaped and dangled in front of her face. Bare feet protruded from her rolled-up jeans and dirt stained her pale yellow T-shirt.

"Felicia?" I said as we crossed the yard toward her.

She turned, glanced over her shoulder, and then stood. "That didn't take long. I thought I'd get at least half of these in the ground before you got here."

Her yard was small but immaculately cared for. Thick, healthy-looking shrubs lined the edge and a pair of shade trees anchored each rear corner. Flowers lined the walkway that led from the back porch to a small circular patio toward the rear of the property, where an umbrella-shaded table and chairs sat.

"It's magnificent," Divya said. "You obviously have a green thumb."

"Got it from my mother. She could grow anything."

"I used to garden," Divya said. "When I was a young girl."

"Really?"

"Nothing like this, but I did like playing in the dirt and loved the fact that you could plant seeds and flowers would appear. I thought it was magic."

Felicia laughed. "In a way it is." She rubbed her hands together and then swatted dirt from the knees of her pants. She looked around her yard. "It's also what I do for therapy." She smiled. "Helps preserve my sanity. And it's cheaper than a psychiatrist."

"Playing in the dirt will do that," I said.

"Would either of you care for some lemonade? I made some fresh about an hour ago and it's nice and cold."

"That's not necessary."

"I'm getting some for myself, so it's no problem."

Felecia invited us to sit at the patio table while she

washed her hands and face. Divya and I settled beneath the umbrella. I opened my briefcase, pulled out the reports that had been faxed over from the hospital, and spread them on the table. Felicia returned, freshly scrubbed and carrying three glasses of lemonade.

She flopped in the chair across from us. "So what did you find out?"

I turned the MRI image of her brain toward her so she could see.

"Is that my brain?"

"Part of it."

"This is unbelievable. It's so clear."

People who have never seen an MRI image are always shocked at the clarity and the minute details exposed by the image. It actually shows more than if you had the organ in your hand. The separation of the various tissues, nerves, and blood vessels is astounding. I remember the first time I saw one. Back in medical school. The difference between those images and the typical X-ray images that I had been used to dealing with was amazing.

"Medical progress," I said. "The MRI has given us a view of the body like we never thought possible."

"It looks very *Star Trek* to me."

"In some ways it is," Divya said.

"Okay, so we know I have a brain," Felicia said. "I assume there's something wrong with it or you wouldn't have come over here to show me the pictures. Right?"

"You might not be able to see this," I said as I used

my ballpoint pen to indicate an area on the image, "but right here there is some swelling."

She studied the image. "If you say so. All I see is something that looks like cauliflower."

I laughed. "That cauliflower is your brain, and right here, this small area, is the origin of the glossopharyngeal nerve. It's one of the twelve cranial nerves. These are the nerves that come from the base of the brain and do things like allowing you to see, hear, smell, and move your facial muscles so you can smile and talk. One of these cranial nerves also controls your heartbeat and blood pressure."

"So what happens when they get swollen?"

"This one, the glossopharyngeal, supplies the throat, ear, and tongue as well as other areas. It helps you speak and swallow and control your tongue, and it also carries sensations from these areas back to the brain. When it becomes swollen or inflamed, as we see here on your MRI, it can cause the deep, aggravating pain you've been having."

"Is that why I get it sometimes when I'm eating or talking on the phone?"

"Exactly. This nerve is involved in both of those activities, so when you eat or talk and the nerve is inflamed, pain can be the result."

"That makes sense." She took a swallow of lemonade. "Does this mean I have to stop eating and talking?"

"I don't think that'll be necessary," I said.

"Good. I like to do both."

"The other thing is that this nerve is also involved in

the functioning of the heart, particularly the rhythm. Sometimes when people have these discomforts the heartbeat slows down. Sometimes dramatically. Sometimes enough to cause dizziness and even loss of consciousness."

"That's why I've been having these dizzy spells?"

"I suspect so. We call this condition glossopharyngeal neuralgia." I smiled. "We have big words for everything, but basically it's a pain in the neck."

Felicia laughed. "You can say that again." She took another sip of her lemonade. "So what do we do about it?"

"Your Holter monitor showed that at times your heart slows down, but not severely so. You had no episodes of long pauses in the rhythm. That means that the likelihood you might actually faint is small."

"That's a relief. A couple of times I thought I might."

"It also means you don't need a pacemaker."

She parked a wayward strand of hair behind her ear. "Pacemaker?"

"That's right," Divya said. "Some people with this have such dramatic changes in their cardiac rhythm that they need the protection of a pacemaker."

"Fortunately, you don't," I said. "We'll start you on medication to help relieve the swelling and discomfort. It's a medicine called gabapentin that's typically used for seizures. It seems to work fairly well in this situation."

"Will that relieve this pain?" She rubbed the side of her neck.

"Are you having discomfort now?" Divya asked.

"I don't know. Maybe. Probably my imagination. Sometimes it feels like it's coming on, but then it doesn't. Other times it sort of zaps me. All of a sudden."

"Let's get the medication started," I said. "In a couple weeks we'll see how you're doing."

Chapter 16

The First Annual Hamptons Health and Fitness Fair opened at eight o'clock sharp with a bit of fanfare. The mayor showed up, as did the chief of police, members of the city council, and Principal Jerry Hyatt. Jill used the microphone and a small amplifier to welcome the crowd of more than two hundred that had gathered just outside the chain-link gate. She then handed the ceremonial scissors to the mayor and he cut through the bright yellow ribbon. The gates swung open. The fair had officially begun

Evan, Divya, and I watched from near the goalposts of the football field and moved out of the way as the crowd surged forward. Most were kids who danced and ran and pleaded with their parents to keep up. The bulk of the rowdy kids headed for the infield, where the obstacle course and other sports venues had been set up. Others flared to the left and right and began visiting the booths that lined either side of the field.

We retreated to the HankMed booth, where fresh coffee awaited. Evan had stopped by Bagel Shack for bagel sandwiches, what appeared to be a half-gallon carton of coffee, and a stack of cups. He grabbed some coffee and immediately headed out to schmooze. Divya began rearranging our supplies.

"Aren't you finished yet?" I asked.

"Finished with what?" she said over her shoulder as she rummaged in one of the two boxes of supplies I had carried from the van.

"Reorganizing everything. You went through all that three times yesterday."

She turned and scowled at me, a pack of four-by-four gauze in her hand. "There's not as much room in here as it looks. I'm simply trying to make things accessible but out of the way." She tossed the gauze to me. "You can help if you want."

I placed the gauze on the edge of the desk. "I thought I was helping by staying out of the way."

She nodded. "Good idea."

I poured a cup of coffee and sat behind the desk. Nothing to do except wait for our first visitor. I suspected it would take a while for all the athletic events to get going, and after that we'd begin seeing bumps, bruises, scrapes, and strains. Turned out it didn't take that long.

A young mother showed up with her five-year-old son who had fallen headlong while racing through the gate and bumped his head. A small bruise and abrasion and of course tears resulted, but it took only a few minutes to clean it up and put a bandage on it. By the time I finished, the bump was forgotten and the boy wanted to get on with the day. His mother thanked us as she was being yanked out of the booth.

Jill stopped by.

"Looks like a good start," I said.

She gazed out toward the field, where the crowds continued to grow. "Better than I thought. Last night I lay there staring at the ceiling thinking that absolutely no one would show up."

"You should've called me. I would've shown up."

"Right. I'm sure you would have."

"I mean, after all, you were already staring at the ceiling."

She gave me a playful punch. "Sometimes you're a pig, you know that?"

"Just trying to be helpful. Cure your insomnia."

"Make yourself useful. Pour me some coffee."

I did and handed it to her. She took a sip.

"Evan brought your favorite bagel sandwiches, too." I nodded toward the bag sitting on one of the exam tables.

"Sometimes I just love him." She opened the bag and took out a wrapped sandwich.

"And the other times?" Divya asked.

"I tolerate him."

"Don't we all?"

Jill unwrapped the sandwich and took a bite. "Mmm. Right now I love him."

"Maybe I'll have one, too," I said.

Jill tossed one my way.

After a few bites, Jill rewrapped the remainder of her bagel and dropped it into her purse. "I'm out of here. Need to go make the rounds and make sure everything is running smoothly."

As soon as Jill left, Evan showed up. Not alone. He had two women in tow. One looked concerned; the other clutched a hand to her chest.

"Dude," Evan said, "you need to see Debbie."

I looked at the woman in pain, who I assumed was Debbie, and asked, "What's the matter?"

She took a breath and winced. "I don't know. I just got this sharp pain. Right here." She pressed her fingers against her chest just to the right of her sternum. "It just happened all of a sudden."

Before I could ask any more questions, Evan launched into who the women were and how he knew them. As if that was relevant. I raised a hand to slow him down, but he ignored me and pressed on. I gave up and waited him out.

I learned that the one with chest pain was Debbie Feiner and her friend was Patricia Masters. They owned a candle, lotion, and potpourri shop in Southampton called Serendipity Scents. Apparently Evan knew them and had convinced them to buy a booth for the health fair. Their booth was just down the row.

With Evan's dissertation out of the way, I directed Debbie to sit on one of the exam tables and adjusted a privacy screen around it while Divya checked her blood pressure. It was normal. I listened to her lungs.

Clear. Heart, too. As I pressed my fingers against her chest, attempting to see if I could reproduce the pain, I detected the telltale signs of subcutaneous emphysema. Nothing else feels like that. It's a crunchy sensation, as if someone had injected glass beads or Rice Krispies just beneath the skin. It's actually trapped air bubbles.

"When did this happen?" I asked.

"Just a few minutes ago. We were blowing up some balloons to decorate our booth and I got this sudden pain."

"So it happened while you were blowing up a balloon?"

She nodded. "Exactly." She took another breath and winced again. "What is it?"

"Let's get an X-ray and then we'll know for sure."

Divya and I rolled our portable unit out of the van and set it up in the middle booth. Having the van here was already proving to be a good idea and our day had just begun.

Debbie's X-ray showed exactly what I expected.

In order for air to leak into the subcutaneous area, there must be a breach in the pulmonary system. It's often seen in people with chronic lung disease, particularly emphysema, where a bleb, basically a blister in the lung, ruptures and the air leaks. This can gather beneath the skin and create subcutaneous emphysema. It's also seen in asthmatics and in some situations that produce what we call barotrauma—lung damage due to pressure. Scuba divers can suffer this. Coughing and sneezing can sometimes make it happen. And blowing up balloons, which causes the pressure inside the chest to increase dramatically, can definitely do it.

The images I had transferred to my laptop revealed that Debbie had a pneumomediastinum. That's a big word for the collection of air in the mediastinum, the area between the lungs where the heart sits. I explained this to her.

"That sounds bad," Evan said.

I gave him a look. One that said he wasn't helping the situation.

"Well, it does," he said.

"So what do we do about it?" Debbie asked. "An operation or something?"

I smiled. "No, you don't need an operation. Both of your lungs are inflated and working fine. This is simply a minor air leak caused by you blowing up the balloons. It'll go away. Might take a few days, but your body will ultimately absorb and remove all the air."

"I guess I should avoid the balloons?"

"Absolutely. For a few weeks anyway. And try not to sneeze."

"Oh, my God, I can't even imagine what that would feel like."

"A little uncomfortable. Sort of like a knife."

She sighed, which caused her to wince again. She brought her hand to her chest. "I guess I shouldn't do that either."

"You're going to be uncomfortable for a few days. I'll give you a prescription for pain meds that'll help some."

"Do I have to go home? Or stay in bed? Anything like that?"

"Not at all. In fact, it's probably better that you stay here at the fair so I can keep an eye on you."

She nodded. "Thank goodness. I'd hate to dump all this on Patricia right here when the weekend is just beginning."

"Don't worry," Patricia said. "I can handle it."

"I know. I'd just hate for that to happen."

I interrupted. "Well, that's a moot point. You can stay and work the booth—just no more balloons."

Debbie stood. "No problem there."

"Either Divya or I will stop by and see you in a while, but in the meantime if anything changes get back here."

"Will do."

"I'll run and pick up your prescription," Patricia said.

"I'll do it," Debbie said.

"No. You rest at the booth. It'll only take me a few minutes."

Debbie nodded and then looked at me. "Thanks for everything."

"Glad we could help," I said.

"I'll walk you guys back to your booth," Evan said.

My brother the gentleman.

Chapter 17

Jill's worries about rain proved to be unfounded. By noon the temperature had risen into the upper eighties and the sky was cloudless, the breeze timid. The best advice would have been to find a shady spot and avoid strenuous physical activity. Not so easy at a health and fitness fair where athletic events were stacked up one after the other. The heat was beginning to exact its price.

Besides the usual bumps and scrapes, Divya and I were now seeing cases of dehydration. Most people were simply sweaty, flushed, and fatigued, a couple slightly dizzy, but no true heat injuries. Most were re-hydrated with glasses of water; only one, an elderly man who wobbled in on his wife's arm, required IV fluids.

The athletic events were in full swing. From where I stood at the entrance of the HankMed booth, I could see the various age groups running the obstacle course, performing the long jump, and racing around the track. I suspected that with all this activity and without a cloud in the sky we would see more cases of dehydration before the day was over.

I decided to track Jill down and suggest that she get an easily accessible water dispenser out in the field for the participants. Divya stayed behind to cover the booth. My first stop was directly across from us at the Hamptons Heritage booth. That's where I found Jill.

"We've been seeing several people with dehydration," I said.

"Here, too."

"Are the only water stations the two refreshment stands?"

"I think so."

"We need more. The kids need to drink more water."

"What'd you have in mind?"

"Let's take a walk down to the obstacle course area."

We waited for a break in the runners so we could cross the track and reach the infield. By the time we got to the obstacle course's starting line, the interschool contests were under way. Each grade from each school had boy and girl teams that vied for ribbons and trophies. The grand prize, a large trophy that sat on a nearby table and gleamed in the sunlight, would go to the school with the best overall score.

School colors were the dress of the day. Right now a line of green-and-white-clad seventh-grade girls stood near the starting line anxiously awaiting their turn. They giggled and high-fived and encouraged each other, saying things like "We're going to trash the competition" and "Keep your focus" and "Let's go crush them." And who said girls aren't as competitive as boys?

"The coaches have been bringing water over," Jill said. She indicated a tray that now held only two water-filled paper cups. The trash can next to it was filled with discarded cups. "But it looks like they might not be keeping up."

"Maybe a couple of those big barrel water dispensers would help," I suggested.

"Yes, they would." She shook her head. "I should have thought of that."

"I don't think anyone predicted it would be this hot today."

"Still . . ." She shrugged. "We have a couple of big orange ones in our booth. I'll get someone to grab them and fill them up." She looked around. "I'll set up another table next to the trophy display and put them there."

"Perfect," I said.

"I'll get the vendors to supply the cups," Jill said. "I'm sure they won't mind."

There were two refreshment stands, one at each end of the field. We walked to the nearest one. It was busy, with four lines of people waiting to buy sodas, hot dogs, hamburgers, and ice cream. I guess even at a health fair you couldn't keep dogs, burgers, and ice cream out.

Jill waved to a man behind the counter. He walked

our way. He wore tan shorts, sandals, and a light blue golf shirt. Jill explained the situation and he readily agreed to donate all the cups she might need.

"I'll run a bunch over there right now," he said. "And I'll check back periodically to make sure you have plenty on hand."

"Thanks," Jill said. "That's a big help."

We then made our way back across the track and along the row of booths in the direction of the Hank-Med booth. About halfway down we ran into Evan, talking with George and Betsy Shanahan.

"Hank. Jill," Betsy said.

"Are you enjoying yourselves?" Jill asked.

"Absolutely. You've done an incredible job."

"Truly remarkable," George said. "Everything is so well organized and seems to be running so smoothly it feels like this has been going on for years."

Jill laughed. "It feels like I've been working on it for years."

"You should be proud of what you've done."

Jill looked around. "None of this could've happened without the support of people like you."

"Next year we'll give even more," Betsy said. "Events like this are so good for the kids and for the entire community."

Evan seemed distracted. He kept looking toward a booth two slots down from where we stood. I followed his gaze. The booth contained half a dozen high-tech massage chairs. Each was occupied and there were a few people loitering around, obviously waiting their turn. The three people working the booth were handing out brochures.

George glanced at his watch. "We'd better get going if we're going to see all the booths before we have to leave."

"We have a barbecue to go to," Betsy said. "George is never late for barbecue."

He laughed and patted his belly. "And I've had practically nothing to eat all day in anticipation."

After they left, Evan headed directly toward the massage chairs. Jill and I followed. The owners of Good Vibrations were two young women. Fit and tanned and wearing white shorts and pink form-fitting Good Vibrations T-shirts, they looked like sisters. They also looked like they could work at Marcy's Bodyworks. Who knows, maybe they had at one time. They greeted Evan with hugs and cheek kisses.

My brother the social butterfly.

Evan introduced Jill and me to Niki and Lisa Norris. They were sisters.

"Thanks for being here," Jill said.

"Are you kidding?" Niki said. "Thanks for having us." She propped an arm on Evan's shoulder. "When Evan stopped by last month and asked if we were interested, we jumped right on it."

Evan beamed.

My brother the salesman.

"We've done more business just today than we do in a week at the store," Lisa said.

"More like two weeks," Niki said.

A chair came free and Evan jumped in it. "I love these things."

Niki laughed. "He's been in the store almost daily the past few weeks."

"And all this time I thought he was working," I said.

"Not daily," Evan said. "Just a few times."

"I'd bet on daily," Lisa said.

Evan rocked back, his legs kicking up as the chair settled into a reclining position. He worked the controls. A faint hum sounded.

"Ah, that's it," Evan said, his voice vibrating with the chair.

"I'll leave him in your hands," I said to Niki and Lisa. "Send him home when you get tired of him."

By midafternoon the temperature had reached the low nineties. No clouds and little breeze left the athletic event participants to the mercy of the sun. Divya and I dealt with the consequences. The dehydration problems we had seen earlier ticked up a notch. We saw at least two dozen people with significant dehydration, cramps, and dizziness. Most could be handled with rest, shade, and a quart of water, but a half dozen required IV fluids.

Around three o'clock a very precocious young man showed up. Patrick Knight was a twelve-year-old black male with long arms and legs, oversized feet, large brown eyes that reminded me of one of those Furby dolls, and an off-the-wall sense of humor. He didn't show up on his own. His mother dragged him over. Apparently against his protests.

"What's the problem?" I asked as mother and son entered the booth.

"He's got all overheated," she said. She was thin, with orange-dyed hair in tight cornrows and tipped braids that hung to her shoulders. She had the same large eyes as her son.

The young man crossed his arms over his chest and stuck his chin out. "Am not."

She thumped the back of his head with a finger. "You tell the doctor here what's going on."

"What's your name?" I asked him.

"Patrick. Patrick Knight. This is my mom. Her name is Rochelle."

"I'm glad to meet you both." I looked at Patrick. "Why don't you hop up here on the table and let me take a look at you."

"I don't have much time."

"Is that right? And where do you have to be?"

He looked at me as if I had asked a ridiculous question. "The long jump. It's going to start in about an hour. I need to stretch out." His chin extended even more. "And I'm going to win."

"So you're pretty good?"

"Lord, yes," Rochelle said. "Just like his daddy. This boy is one heck of an athlete."

"What sports do you play?"

"All of them," Patrick said. "Baseball, basketball,

track, and football." He looked toward his mother. "She don't like me playing football, but that's my favorite."

"Why don't you tell me what you've been feeling?"

"Nothing. I'm fine."

"Patrick Henry Knight, you tell him right now. You hear me?"

He shook his head and rolled his eyes. "I knew I shouldn't of told you." Patrick nodded his head toward his mother. "She makes a big deal out of everything."

"That's what mothers are supposed to do," I said.

"I reckon. Anyway it's not much. I had some cramps in my legs and got a little bit light-headed."

"What were you doing when this happened?"

"We'd just finished some races and I was standing around."

"Let me guess. Not drinking much water?"

"That's right," Rochelle said. "I told him he wasn't drinking enough."

"Any headaches or nausea or blurred vision or anything like that?" I asked.

"None of that."

I smiled. "You wouldn't tell me anyway, would you?"

He looked at me. "Probably not."

I gave Patrick a quick examination and found everything was normal. His lungs were clear, his heart rhythm steady and regular, his abdomen soft, and no tenderness in his legs.

"You're a little dehydrated."

"Okay, so I'll drink more water. Then go do the long jump." He slid off the table. "Thanks."

"Not so fast," I said, grabbing his arm. "Four glasses. You have to drink four glasses of water before I let you leave." I patted the exam table.

He jumped back up on the table. "I can do that standing on my head."

"A little hard to drink in that position, don't you think?"

"You're funny." He looked at his mother. "I didn't know doctors could be funny. He's a lot funnier than that guy you take me to."

Rochelle shook her head. "See what I have to put up with?"

I filled a twelve-ounce plastic cup from the two-gallon water dispenser we had sitting on the corner of the desk and handed it to Patrick. He chugged it, so I refilled it.

"A little slower."

"Man, come on, I've got to do some jumping."

"Dr. Lawson?"

I looked up to see Jonathan Wiggins. He owned Wiggins Waters, a boutique water store in Southampton. I had seen his booth earlier. Down at the far end of the field. He had a hand truck stacked with four cases of his branded mineral water.

"Can you use some mineral water?" he asked.

"Absolutely," Divya said.

"I'll leave you a couple of cases. I'm taking the others over to the Hamptons Heritage booth." He glanced that way and then back at me. "With all this heat we've been doing a bang-up business and I figured you guys could probably use some. On the house, of course."

"That's very kind," Divya said. "We don't want to take your entire inventory, though."

"No problem there. I sent my son over to the warehouse to load up the truck."

Jonathan removed two of the cardboard boxes and placed them on the exam table. He tore one open while I opened the other.

He lifted a plastic bottle filled with yellow-tinged water. "This one is lemon-lime, and the ones you got there are raspberry. There's lots of magnesium and potassium in them."

"I'll take a raspberry," Patrick said.

I handed him one and then asked Rochelle, "And you?"

"I'd love a lemon-lime."

"Here you go," Jonathan said as he handed her a bottle. "I need to get these over to the hospital booth. I'll bring some more by as soon as my son gets back."

"Thanks."

"Man, this is good," Patrick said. "When I get back from winning the long jump I'll try lemon-lime."

"You seem pretty sure you're going to win," I said.

"He probably will," Rochelle said. "He can do just about anything he puts his mind to. Athletics, even his schoolwork. The problem is keeping him from breaking his neck."

"You're saying he's a little rambunctious."

"That hardly seems strong enough. Been that way his whole life. When he was five—when we lived down in Florida—he tried to jump off the garage roof. Had the corners of a towel tied together thinking that'd be a good parachute. Five years old. Can you imagine?"

Actually I could. Maybe not at five, but around age twelve I talked Evan into climbing on the roof with me. We had parachutes made of bedsheets. Evan went first. Cracked a bone in his foot. I thought about not jumping as I stood there watching him roll around on the ground, foot pulled to his chest. But that wasn't an option. I couldn't chicken out after Evan had jumped. So I prayed nothing bad would happen and off I went. Nothing broke, but it wasn't nearly as much fun as I'd thought it would be. I had envisioned us floating to the ground, not dropping like sacks of potatoes. I suspected Patrick had had the same vision.

"He's always banging and bruising himself," Rochelle continued. "That's why his knees and back and elbows hurt all the time."

Patrick rolled his eyes again. "See what I'm saying? She worries about everything."

Rochelle looked at me. "The boy's had growing pains his whole life. Of course, he won't complain about it. I have to ask, but half the time he won't tell me. I remember once he sprained his shoulder really bad playing football and didn't tell me about it for a week." She glared at her son. "Fact is, he didn't tell me at all. His coach did."

"That's because you'd make a big deal out of it and I wouldn't get to play."

"Hank?" Divya said. She nodded toward the front of the booth.

I turned to see a woman helping a middle-aged man. He had his arm draped over her shoulders and his gait was unsteady.

Patrick jumped off the exam table. "Dude, looks like you better lay down here."

I agreed with Patrick and helped the man onto the table.

"What happened?"

"He's overheated. He's been out there running around like a fool. I told him he was too old to chase the kids."

"I might've overdone it a bit," the man said.

I gave him a quick examination and found that other than dehydration he was fine. I started an IV and began pumping him full of fluids.

Patrick watched everything, his eyes getting even bigger. "That's so cool," he said.

"Maybe you'll be a doctor someday," I said.

"If I'm not an NFL quarterback I just might."

Lack of confidence wasn't one of Patrick's faults.

Chapter 18

Evan was in full schmooze mode. After spending twenty minutes in the massage chair and telling Niki and Lisa he would return later for another session, he made the circuit. He visited most of the booths that circled the track, asking if anyone needed anything and thanking them for signing up. The only problem he encountered was one booth where the power had died. He called Jill and she sent her volunteer electrician by. The problem was a disconnected cable two booths over. A reconnection and a duct tape wrap corrected it.

Evan soon reached Rachel Fleming's booth. The back flaps of the booth were open, revealing two brightly painted vans parked just behind. Rachel stood next to a blue one with oversized wheels and an attached Jet Ski trailer, talking with a family of four. Mom, dad, two sons in the twelve-year-old range. She saw Evan and nodded, holding up a finger to tell him she'd be there in a minute.

It was more like ten, but after the family left Rachel walked back into the booth.

"How's business?" Evan asked.

"Amazing. I nailed down two orders today and a dozen appointments for next week." She brushed a wayward strand of hair from her face. "I'm glad you talked me into this."

"Do you have time for coffee. Or ice cream?"

"No. I'm here by myself the rest of the day. Rain check?"

"Tomorrow. An ice cream date."

"You're on."

"Cool."

Evan left and completed his circuit, ending up at Good Vibrations. Still busy. Two of the chairs were occupied by giggling teenage girls. One blonde, one brunette, both wearing cutoff jeans and halter tops.

"Looks like they're having fun," Evan said to Niki.

"They're ripped," Lisa said.

Evan looked at them again, now noticing that their eyes were a little glazed. The brunette said something to the blonde that Evan couldn't make out and they both burst into laughter.

"See what I mean? Stoned and headed toward stupid."

Evan walked over. "How are you young ladies doing?"

"Peachy," the blonde said. More laughter.

"More like strawberry," the brunette replied. Even more laughter.

"You look stoned."

"You think?" the blonde said.

"No, we're not," the brunette said. "We're baked. Totally."

"Totally," the blonde agreed.

"Time's up," Niki said.

"Dude, we're just getting relaxed," the brunette said.

Niki helped her out of the chair. She staggered, bumping into Evan. He caught her.

"Whoa. Easy," Evan said.

"See how relaxed I am?"

"Not the word I would use," Niki said.

"Come on, Katy," the blonde said. "Let's go somewhere fun."

"Want to have some fun?" Evan said. "I know a cool place."

"Who are you?"

"Evan."

She propped one hand on her hip. "I'm Gloria. This is Katy." She eyed Evan up and down. "You look like a cool dude."

Katy was now upright. "So where's this fun place?"

"Just down the row here. My brother's booth. You need to see it."

"Cool, dude. Let's go."

Jonathan Wiggins, true to his word, returned with four cases of his mineral water. As Divya and I were opening the boxes, Danielle and Angela showed up. Dan-

ielle wore tight black athletic shorts and a white T-shirt
with what appeared to be a red surfboard on the front.
Hard to be sure with her sling strap partially covering
it. Angela wore a blue dress and a broad straw hat. She
maneuvered her walker like a pro.

"You're getting good with that," I said.

"Not much choice. I'll be glad when I can get rid
of it."

"Patience."

"You sound like those rehab thugs."

Danielle laughed. "They came by this morning. Apparently they kicked up her program to the next level."

"The next level? They nearly killed me."

"I doubt it," I said. "They simply want to get you
back to your old self."

"Don't talk about my age." She gave me one of her
sly grins.

I dragged the chair from behind the desk. "Here. Sit
down."

Once Angela settled in the chair, I offered her and
Danielle mineral water. They each chose raspberry.

"I thought it would be good to get Grandma out and
about, so we decided to come by and see how the fair
is going," Danielle said.

"Busy," I said.

"Looks like it. The parking lot is nearly full. I had to let
Grandma out and then go find a spot. Way in the back."

"How's your shoulder feeling?"

She moved it back and forth. "Better. It's a lot less
stiff and sore."

"Let me take a look."

"Sure."

I tested her range of motion and palpated over her AC joint. More mobile and less tender. "It's getting there."

"I think I'll make the meet."

"I never doubted it," I said.

"Me either," Angela added.

"You can probably dump the sling tomorrow or the next day. If you're careful and don't overdo it."

"Thank goodness. I'm tired of being one-armed."

I heard giggles and turned to see Evan with two young girls. High schoolers. Hair disheveled. Eyes glazed. Pupils dilated. What had Evan gotten into now?

"Is this your brother?" one of the girls asked.

"Yes," Evan said. "This is Hank." He indicated the two girls. "This is Katy and Gloria. They're sisters." He then introduced Divya, Angela, and Danielle.

Danielle gave Evan a look. One that said: "What's this all about?"

"I thought Katy and Gloria should meet you," Evan said to me. "See the new van. That kind of thing."

My brother. Mr. Sneaky.

The fact that these two young ladies were on something was obvious. Even to Evan. And to his credit he had tricked them into coming to the booth. I suspected that telling them they needed help would have run them off, but dragging them down here with a carrot rather than a stick worked.

"You don't look like brothers," Gloria said.

"Maybe one of you was adopted," Katy said.

Both girls burst into laughter.

Gloria's eyes widened and she looked at me. "Wouldn't that be like so gnarly? Finding out you were adopted?"

"Neither of us was adopted," I said. "And we really are brothers, though sometimes I ask myself why."

That brought more laughter from the girls.

Katy's eyes seemed to finally land on Danielle. She hesitated a beat, and then her hand went to her mouth. "Get out of here. Are you who I think you are?"

"Depends," Danielle said. "Who do you think I am?"

Katy elbowed Gloria. "Are you believing this, dude?"

"Believing what?" Gloria still didn't have a clue.

"Danielle Delaney."

Gloria looked around. "Where?"

Katy pointed to Danielle. "Right there."

Gloria seemed to focus on Danielle for a minute. "Are you sure? Why would she be here?"

"Everybody has to be somewhere," Danielle said. "Here is as good a place as any."

"This is so like totally cool," Gloria said.

"Totally," Katy echoed.

"Will you sign something for me?" Gloria asked. She looked around and then at herself. She held her right arm out. "Maybe my arm."

Danielle laughed. "I think we can do better than that."

The two girls stared at her, waiting. Or maybe they hadn't understood. Hard to tell which.

"Give me your addresses, and I'll send each of you a signed photo."

The girls laughed, Katy jumping up and down. "That would be radically awesome."

"Speaking of radically awesome," I said, "what have you girls taken today?"

"Who said we took anything?" Gloria said. She glanced at her sister and again they both giggled.

"I didn't say that," Katy said.

"Me either," Gloria agreed.

More laughter.

I stared at them, waiting. Finally the giggling died.

"Okay, okay," Katy said. "It's no biggie. We took some magic pills." She laughed. "Way magic."

"How old are you?" I asked.

"Seventeen," Katy said. "My sister is sixteen."

"What did you take?"

"I told you," Katy said. "Magic pink pills."

There was that feeling I hate again. The one where the hair on your neck snaps to attention and a cold feeling slides down your spine.

"What kind of pink pills?" I asked.

Katy looked at me as if I was crazy. "Little round pink pills, dude."

I smiled. "I meant what was in them?"

"I don't know."

"We didn't do well in chemistry class," Gloria said.

"Like totally bad," Katy agreed.

They both laughed hysterically.

"Didn't do a *CSI* analysis either," Gloria said.

"We just took them," Katy said.

"Just like that?" I asked. "Someone gives you a pill and you swallow it?"

They stared at me as if I was from another planet.

"Well, duh," Katy said. "That's what you do with pills."

"And they didn't give them to us," Gloria said. "We had to like buy them. Five bucks each."

"They who?"

They stared at me, and then Katy said, "They what?"

"They. The people you bought the pills from."

"Oh. This cool couple."

The hair on my neck stiffened a bit more. "Where'd you see them?"

"In the parking lot."

"When?"

"Dude, what's with all the questions?" Katy asked.

"If you want some, we can hook you up," Gloria added.

"With this couple?"

"True story," Katy said. She staggered a step, caught herself, and laughed.

Divya handed each of them a bottle of mineral water. "This might help."

Katy held up the bottle and stared at the pinkish liquid inside. "This is so neat. Look at the color." She twisted off the cap. No easy task for her, but she managed. She took a gulp. "Whoa. This is rich."

Gloria took a sip of hers. "Way rich, dude." Then she giggled. "Maybe we could make this stuff into pills?"

"Radical," Katy said. "We could call it Raspberry Quick."

"Raspberry Quick?" I asked.

Katy looked at me. "Yeah. The ones we took were Strawberry Quick. Raspberry ones would be like the ultimate."

"Not only make you feel good, but they're good for you," Gloria said.

"How so?" I asked.

Gloria gave me a quizzical look. I was now officially from another planet. "Dude? Are you serious? Strawberry? Fruit group? The food pyramid?"

At first I thought she was joking. Or maybe I hoped she was. But the seriousness on her face revealed that she wasn't.

"Somehow I don't think this is what they had in mind when they developed the food groups."

"Maybe they should have," Katy said.

"True story," added Gloria.

"Tell me about this couple," I said. "The ones that sold you the Strawberry Quick."

"What about them?" Gloria asked.

"Do you know their names?"

Gloria shook her head, but Katy said, "Pete something. And her name was . . . I can't remember."

I glanced at Divya and then back to the girls. "Erin?"

"Yeah. I think that's right." Katy now focused on me. "Do you know them?"

"No. What did they look like?"

"She's cool," Gloria said. "Skinny and hot. I wish I was that skinny."

"And she always has the coolest jeans," Katy added.

"She has long hair," Gloria said. "Dark. Nearly to her waist."

"The dude's hair is long, too," Katy said. "He has like this totally stoked ponytail."

"That sounds like the couple we saw at the beach," Danielle said.

"It does," Evan agreed.

"What couple?" I asked.

Evan told the story of the three stoned boys who had harassed him at the beach. "I saw them a little later talking to a couple that sounds like these two. It looked like they bought something from them."

"The beach?" Katy said. "That's probably them. We hook up with them there sometimes."

"And I saw them again yesterday," Evan said. "Also at the beach. But they sped off before I could get their license plate number."

Probably a good thing. I'm not sure Evan should get involved with this.

"Is the doctor here?"

I looked up. A woman stood at the entrance to the tent, her hand firmly clamped on the upper arm of a young girl.

"I'm Dr. Lawson," I said.

"Can you take a look at my daughter?"

"What's the matter?"

"This." She extended a plastic baggie toward me. It held two pink pills.

"That's them," Katy said. "They're so much fun."

I suppose I should have been shocked by Katy's openness. As if taking illegal drugs was no big deal. As if it was almost expected. A big difference from when I was in school. Back then those things were hidden and denied. A little water could mask the theft of alcohol from a parent's liquor cabinet. Beer drinking and marijuana smoking took place in private.

That's all changed.

As Principal Hyatt told me, the students now sit in their cars in the school parking lot and get stoned. They come to class intoxicated. They don't seem to respect or fear any type of authority. Like Katy and Gloria. They seemed oblivious to the fact that what they had done was illegal. Not to mention dangerous.

The woman glared at Katy and then looked back to me. "She's acting weird. Out of it. And I found these in her purse."

"Where you had no right to look."

See what I mean?

"You're fifteen, young lady," the woman said, giving her daughter a shake. "You don't get to make the rules yet."

Fifteen, I thought. So young. She looked more mature, but she was still only a child.

"What's your name?" I asked.

"Rapunzel."

"Really? You don't look like a Rapunzel." I can play this game, too.

"Whatever. What difference does it make?"

The woman rolled her eyes and sighed. "Meghan. Her name is Meghan. I'm Millie Samuels. Her mother."

"Okay, Meghan or Rapunzel," I said. "Why don't you sit here on the exam table?"

"I'm fine. Just leave me alone."

Millie glared at her. "Get up there now. Do what he says or you'll be grounded for a year. You hear me?"

"How could I not?" Meghan yanked her arm free and climbed up on the table. She crossed her arms over her chest. "Okay, I'm here."

My exam showed that her blood pressure and heart rate were elevated slightly, pupils dilated and poorly reactive, and reflexes hyperactive. The signs of amphetamine use.

"When did you take the pills?"

She looked toward the floor.

"It's important," I said. "You're showing signs of amphetamine intoxication and I need to know if you're coming down or still heading up."

"I don't remember."

"Then I'll have to send you over to Hamptons Heritage's ER for blood testing."

"You can't do that."

"I can," Millie said. "And I will."

"Actually your mother can, but she doesn't have to," I said. "I simply make a call and sign a document and I can hold you in the hospital for up to three days."

She looked at me. "No."

Gloria chimed in. "That's so Nazi, dude."

"Totally," Katy said.

"And the same goes for you two," I said to Gloria and Katy. "I can hold all three of you if I think it's in your best interest."

"That's too radical for words," Katy said.

"Not to mention totally random and mean," Gloria added. She locked her arms across her chest, her chin jutting toward me.

I looked back at Meghan/Rapunzel. "You see, we physicians have an obligation to take care of sick folks even when they refuse to listen to reason. What that means to you is that if I feel your life or health is in danger from drugs or from some psychiatric condition I can hold you against your will until it's all straightened out."

"Mom?"

Millie held up her hands. "Don't look to me, young lady. You always want to be treated like an adult, so act like one and answer his questions."

"Three hours. I took one pill three hours ago."

"Where did you get them?"

She glanced at her mother and then down. "I don't remember."

"I see. Excuse me a second."

As I walked out toward the HankMed van to be out of earshot, I flipped open my phone and made a call. Ten minutes later, a patrol car pulled up next to the booth and Sergeant Willard McCutcheon and Officer

Tommy Griffin stepped out. I introduced them and they flashed their badges. Now Meghan, Katy, and Gloria seemed nervous. I was glad something had finally grabbed their attention.

McCutcheon listened attentively to Gloria, Katy, Meghan, Evan, and Danielle, each telling their story about the mysterious couple. Griffin scribbled notes while McCutcheon asked questions. Each of the kids seemed to answer without hesitation. Fear is a great motivator. Finally he straightened his shoulders and hooked his thumbs in his belt.

"Okay, here's the deal. Meghan, you can go with your mother. If it's okay with Dr. Lawson." I nodded. "Gloria and Katy, I want you to call your parents to come pick you up." Katy started to protest, but he waved her away. "No way you're going to leave here by yourselves. So either you call your parents or I will. You choose."

"Or you can ride home in the back of our squad car," Griffin added.

"That might work," McCutcheon said. "We could pull right up to your house. Let the entire neighborhood see you in the backseat. Caged in like a criminal. We can arrange that if that's what you want."

All their drug-induced joy was gone. Their shoulders drooped in resignation.

"Okay," Katy mumbled. She pulled her cell phone from the back pocket of her jeans.

"Hank," McCutcheon said. "A word?"

We walked out behind the booth, near the van.

"We'll snoop around the area, but I doubt we'll find much since all our guys are in uniform. Tomorrow I'll have some undercover guys sniffing around. Hopefully we'll find these clowns."

"Sounds good."

"Wish we had more to go on, but at least the descriptions I just heard match what Kevin Moxley told us. It helps that everyone saw the same couple." He looked back toward the booth where Gloria stood close to Katy, whose head was down, phone pressed to one ear. "This world is all sideways."

True story, as Katy and Gloria would say.

McCutcheon and Griffin waited until Jillian Weber, the girls' mother, arrived and then had a no-nonsense talk with her. The sisters cowered as their mother fumed. She listened attentively to McCutcheon, casting an occasional scowl at her daughters. I then explained the drug, or rather drugs, that they were taking in those innocent-looking pink pills.

Jillian spun toward her daughters. Her anger, peppered with a healthy dose of fear, I imagine, erupted. "How could you be so stupid? Put some chemical you bought from some lowlife in your bodies? Why not simply shoot yourselves?" Her lips quivered. "You weren't raised that way."

"But, Mom—," Katy began

"Don't you dare try to make an excuse. Wait until your father hears about this."

"Please," Gloria said, "don't tell him. We won't do it again. We promise."

"I'm not going to tell him," Jillian said. "You are. He's going to be so hurt and disappointed." A sob caught in her throat. "He works hard. Gives you girls everything. And this is how you thank him? Thank me?"

"Mom—"

She held up a hand. "Not another word. You hear me?"

Jillian thanked me for taking care of her daughters and for explaining everything to her, and McCutcheon for not arresting them, adding that "a night in jail might do them some good." She then herded them toward the parking lot.

I wouldn't want to be one of the Weber girls. Looked like they were in for a rough evening.

Chapter 19

"You both look delightful," Angela said. "You'll be the hit of the party."

Evan and Danielle each did a three-sixty spin, the capes of their spy costumes flaring around them. Danielle was a little more graceful than Evan, but at least this time he didn't knock anything over.

After leaving the health fair, Evan and Danielle stopped by the costume shop to pick out a matching outfit for Danielle. Divya and I brought Angela to Shadow Pond with us, and while she and Divya chatted I began dinner. Yes, me. Nothing fancy. Not an Evan dinner for sure. I opted for Caesar salad, spaghetti with marinara sauce, and garlic toast.

The sauce, which came from a jar, though I added some ground beef, sausage, and extra garlic, simmered on the stove, its aroma pulling a growl from my stomach. I had somehow missed lunch and Wiggins Water, no matter how good it is, will carry you only so far.

I glanced at my watch. Jill was running late. Again. She's usually the most punctual person I know, but the health fair had knocked her schedule off track for months. After the fair closed this afternoon, she'd had a vendors' meeting followed by a meeting with the security personnel who would watch over the booths tonight.

Danielle did another turn and glided over to where Angela sat in a wingback chair, sipping wine.

"Grandma, I wish you would come to the party," Danielle said.

Angela waved a hand toward her. "I'd be a drag. Parties are for youngsters."

"But I don't want you sitting home alone on the Fourth of July."

"I'll be fine."

"You know you're welcome to come with us," I said. "We'd love it if you did."

"You're just saying that."

"I mean it. It would be fun. If for no other reason than the fireworks. I understand Nathan Zimmer is planning a huge display. Out over the ocean."

"Really?" Angela said. "That must be costing him a bundle."

"He can afford it," Evan said.

"It's pocket change to him," Divya said.

"I do love fireworks," Angela said.

"Then come," I said. "You'll enjoy it."

"I'll think about it."

"Don't think, just do," Danielle said.

"But I don't have a costume."

"That's easy to fix," Evan said. "We'll go back by the shop on Monday."

"I won't be a spy," Angela said. "Or one of those highway robbers you talked about."

Danielle laughed. "Actually, Grandma, I think you'd have been an excellent spy. Highway robber, too."

"What are you trying to say?"

"That you're clever and witty and can do just about anything."

"Not that I'm a larcenous old fool?"

"I would never say that. Especially the fool part."

"They have some wonderful colonial ball gowns," Divya said. "You would look marvelous in one of them."

"You think?"

"Absolutely. But maybe I should take you. I'm not sure you want Evan picking your costume for you."

"He picked mine," Danielle said.

"But that was easy. You'd look good in anything."

"That's not true."

"Really?" Divya asked. "Let's see a show of hands."

We all raised a hand.

Jill walked in. She stopped in midstride and looked at us. "What's this about?"

I explained.

She raised her hand. "Then I'll make it unanimous."

I popped the garlic toast into the oven and dropped the pasta into the pot of boiling water and twenty minutes later we all gathered at the dinner table. Everyone said the spaghetti was excellent. I think they were just being nice. But then again, it wasn't bad.

The conversation returned to Nathan's party.

"I think you should come," Jill said to Angela. "It'll be fun. A true Hamptons event."

"I know. I just don't want to be in the way."

"You won't be," I said. "And if you get tired and want to leave, we'll take you home."

"I wouldn't want to spoil your evening, dear."

Jill laughed. "Are you kidding? Knowing Hank, he'll be looking for an exit after half an hour."

"Funny," I said.

"No, true."

"And Evan and I will be your bodyguards," Danielle said.

"How could I refuse that? My own spies."

"Then it's settled," I said. "You're coming."

Angela sighed. "Okay. I'll do it."

"We'll hit the costume shop Monday morning," Divya said.

With that decided, the conversation turned to the health fair. Jill was thrilled. Everything had run smoothly with no real hiccups. The turnout surpassed expectations and the vendors and booth renters reported brisk sales of their products.

"Rachel Fleming signed contracts for two new vehicles today," Evan said. "She also said she set a dozen appointments for the next couple of weeks."

"Jonathan Wiggins completely sold out of his mineral water," Jill said.

"What he didn't give away," I said.

Jill nodded. "He's a good guy, and he's always supported the clinic. He also asked if I'd put him on the list for a booth next year."

"I guess the only negative was the kids we saw on drugs," Divya said.

"It's amazing," Angela said. "Today's kids are different. I know when Danielle was growing up she wasn't exposed to all the things teenagers see now."

"I get the impression that in her case it wouldn't have mattered," I said.

Danielle laughed. "That's true. I was always the jock chick. Sports don't leave much time for trouble."

"I can't believe they were selling that stuff right there at the fair," Jill said. "Seems incredibly brazen to me."

"It is," I said. "From everyone's description it seems to me that they would stand out in the crowd. I mean her long hair and his ponytail?"

"Not to mention selling at school and the beach," Divya said. "Not exactly dark corners."

"They've been lucky," I said. "But I'd put my money on Sergeant McCutcheon. He seems like a bulldog to me."

"I wouldn't want him after me," Evan said. "He sure scared Katy and Gloria Weber."

"That he did," Divya said. "He even scared me, and I didn't do anything."

"But you look devious," Evan said.

Divya raised an eyebrow and pointed her fork at him. "You want to rephrase that?"

"You might want to reconsider," I said to Evan. "She does have a sharp instrument."

Chapter 20

I got up early Sunday morning and went for a run at the beach. As I drove over, I listened to the weather report. Not good. Today was going to be even hotter than yesterday. As I ran I watched the sun rise into a perfectly clear sky. There was little breeze. By the time I finished my run, sweat plastered my T-shirt to my chest.

Didn't bode well for the day. I had visions of stretcher after stretcher of the overheated and dehydrated.

When I got back home the aroma of bacon greeted me. Evan was in the kitchen preparing breakfast.

"How do you want your eggs?" he asked.

"Whatever you're having is fine with me."

"Scrambled it is." He began cracking eggs into a bowl.

"It's going to be another hot one." I stripped off my T-shirt. "In fact it already is."

Evan added a little milk to the eggs and began beating them with a fork. "Jonathan Wiggins said he would stock his booth with extra cases of his mineral water today. He said if we needed any just let him know and he'll bring it by."

"Jill has already arranged to have more water stations than we had yesterday, so hopefully everything will be better."

Evan dumped the eggs into a skillet. "I wouldn't count on it."

I hoped he was wrong.

Turned out he was right.

For the first hour, things at the HankMed booth were quiet, but they picked up after that. By eleven a.m. the temperature was soaring and we began seeing our first cases of dehydration. Mostly kids and mostly minor. Wiggins Water became the treatment of choice.

The kids seemed to like the mineral water more than the adults did. I thought that was odd, since it wasn't loaded with sugar and caffeine like those energy drinks that are everywhere. And people want to know why kids can't concentrate and why they act out in school.

Jill stopped by a couple of times. She actually had little to do, as everything seemed to be going smoothly. A testament to her organizational skills. I told her that.

"You doubted me?" she asked.

"Never. Just that the first year of anything is usually buggy."

"It helps to have the right volunteers," she said.

"And finding those people was your job. So, good job."

"I could stay and listen to that all day, but unfortunately I'd better go make the rounds again so everything will keep running smoothly."

Divya and I continued seeing the usual minor stuff—bumps and scrapes and even a dislocated little finger. An eight-year-old boy who fell while racing around the track. A painful injury for sure, but mostly very scary-looking. To see your finger angle out in an odd direction is frightening. As it was for the boy. His tears evaporated when I tugged and snapped it back in place. The pain gone and the finger mobile again, he wiped his tears away with the back of his hand.

"Let's get an X-ray done, but I bet it'll be okay."

"Are you sure?" his mother asked. "It looked like it was broken."

"These dislocations usually look worse than they are. There's almost never a fracture involved."

I was right. No fracture. The boy was fascinated by the X-ray of his hand and his mother was relieved that the only thing required would be a splint for a few weeks. I arranged for them to follow up with an orthopedist and they headed out, the mother promising ice cream.

By noon, the temperature approached ninety and what breeze there was offered little relief. Jonathan Wiggins dropped off more of his mineral water. Divya was finishing up with an elderly couple who had come in for respite from the heat when Principal Hyatt showed up. The couple had each finished a bottle of Wiggins Water, and Divya handed them two more as they left, telling them to stay in the shade.

"Another hot one," Hyatt said.

"Yes, it is," I said.

"Mind if I grab one?" Hyatt asked, indicating the case of mineral water.

"Please do."

He chose a lemon-lime. He twisted off the cap, took a couple of swallows, and then examined the label. "This is good. I've never tried it before."

"It's popular," I said.

"I'd suspect it'll be even more popular after this weekend," Divya said. "Jonathan Wiggins said it was selling so fast he couldn't keep stocked."

"He's been donating some to us and to the Hamptons Heritage booth."

"That right?" Hyatt asked. He took another swig. "I'll stop by and see him. Thank him for his generosity." He propped a hip against one of the exam tables. "I had a talk with the Weber family last night."

"Oh?"

"Jillian called. She told me about the girls. Katy is one of our juniors. Gloria's a sophomore."

"How'd it go?"

"Heated. Bill, the girls' father, was furious. Understandably so. His initial reaction was to put them in rehab. Jillian tried to talk him down, but he wouldn't listen, so she called me."

"The life of a high school principal."

He nodded.

I knew it wasn't the life of most principals. Most saw their obligations end at the schoolhouse door. Not Hyatt. He took every kid to heart. Maybe too much so, but that's the way he was. His reputation told me that that was the only way he could do things. So he often found himself in the midst of family dramas.

"But once things cooled down, we made some progress. The bottom line is that Katy and Gloria are good kids. They do well in school and have a very bright future. Bill and Jillian have done a good job raising them. Instilled all the right values. When I finally convinced Bill of that, things smoothed out."

"So the girls aren't going to boot camp?" Divya asked.

Hyatt shook his head. "They simply made a mistake. Folded to peer pressure. Had never done that before. Or so they said."

"The excuse of every teenager," I said.

Hyatt rubbed his chin. "True. But I think Katy and Gloria are different. Don't get me wrong—I've had hundreds of students look me in the eye and lie. I've even been fooled before. But after all the years I've been at this I've developed a sort of internal lie detector. It's not perfect, but it's pretty good."

Experience will do that. Physicians develop the same sense. After a few years of treating patients you develop a sense for when they are being truthful and when they are holding back, or making something up, or maybe simply telling you what they think you want to hear.

It might seem more logical to lie to your high school principal than to your doctor. After all, with the principal you are often in some sort of trouble when you visit his office. Such visits are rarely social and are usually more disciplinary in nature. Lying to protect yourself or your friends, though still wrong, is completely understandable. But lying to your doctor? Why would someone do that?

There are many reasons. Not admitting your own failures or weaknesses is one. Something that is never easy to do. Things like yes, you are still smoking or drinking too much or no, you're not doing your daily exercise or no, you aren't taking your meds every day as you know you should. Some see this as disappointing their doctor and that makes them uncomfortable.

Then there's the fear factor. Fear that your doctor might uncover something awful. If you don't tell him about the symptoms you fear most he won't find that awful thing. Symptoms like shortness of breath, chest pain, dizziness, abdominal pain, and a host of others go unmentioned, even denied.

It's the mental equivalent of closing your eyes, covering your ears, and saying, "La-la-la-la, I can't hear you."

Not smart, but common.

So doctors, principals, cops, and many other so-called authority figures learn to spot lies.

"The solution we came to was for the girls to promise to never do drugs again and for them to have random drug tests anytime their parents want," Hyatt said.

"The girls agreed to that?" Divya asked.

"Not sure they really had a choice. Bill agreed not to punish or ground them for this episode if they agreed to the testing."

"That sounds reasonable to me," I said.

"I think they'll do fine," Hyatt said. He finished his mineral water and tossed the empty into the recycle box in the corner. "I also spoke with Sergeant McCutcheon this morning. He has six undercover guys here today, including Officer Griffin and himself. Maybe he'll grab the dealers."

"If they come back today," I said.

Hyatt walked to the front of the tent and looked out toward the infield. "Bet they will." He turned back toward us. "They see this as a rich market. Full of potential customers. Greed will get them caught."

"I hope you're right."

"Let me know if any of my other students show up on that stuff."

"Will do. And McCutcheon."

"What about McCutcheon?"

The voice came from outside the booth. I looked up as McCutcheon and Griffin stepped around the corner. They looked like tourists. Khaki shorts and Hawaiian shirts, McCutcheon's white and green surfboards on a yellow background, Griffin's dark blue with red and green flowers. The world of the undercover cop.

"And don't say a word about *Hawaii Five-O*," McCutcheon said.

"Wouldn't dream of it," I said. "Even if it does fit."

He laughed. "Been a long time since either of us went undercover. This is the best we could come up with."

"You make a cute couple," Divya said.

"Not you, too."

"We caught a little grief from the other guys this morning," Griffin said.

"But you'll blend in, and that's what counts," Hyatt said.

Chapter 21

"Dr. Lawson?"

I finished wrapping a sprained ankle with an elastic bandage. A middle schooler who didn't exactly nail the landing on the long jump. I told the boy's father to keep his son's foot elevated and iced. Divya handed him a baggie filled with ice.

"Will do." Then to his son I said, "Looks like no more running and jumping for you today."

The boy frowned. "Why did this have to happen today? I was in second place."

"That's pretty good," I said.

"I'd win if it wasn't for Patrick. He won yesterday, too."

"Patrick Knight?" Divya asked.

"Yeah. You know him?"

"We met him yesterday."

"He's good," the boy said.

"So I hear," I said.

The boy hobbled over to his father. "I can't beat him in anything."

"Stick with it," the man said. "You will." He nodded to me. "Thanks."

As they left Evan and Danielle showed up.

"What mischief have Evan R. Lawson and Mata Hari, the superspies, been into?" Divya asked.

"We've been doing the fund-raising walk," Danielle said.

"How many laps so far?" I asked.

"Thirty-two."

"Eight miles? You got my brother to walk eight miles?"

"On those legs?" Divya nodded toward Evan.

Evan wore a pair of black athletic shorts and a white T-shirt. Danielle had on similar shorts with a light green tank top.

"What's wrong with my legs?"

"Nothing a few trips to Marcy's Bodyworks wouldn't help."

"He's been doing great," Danielle said. "In fact he can actually walk and schmooze at the same time." She laughed.

"Evan can schmooze in his sleep," I said.

"Are you guys finished?" Evan said.

"I was going to ask you the same thing."

"We're shooting for fifty laps," Danielle said.

"Don't overdo it," I said.

"It is hot out there." Evan looked around. "Do you have any more of Jonathan's magic water?"

"In the box there," I said.

Evan grabbed a pair of the raspberry ones and handed one to Danielle.

After resting for twenty minutes and downing two bottles of Wiggins Water, Evan and Danielle returned to the track to complete their laps. A few laps later they hooked up with George and Betsy Shanahan. Evan introduced them to Danielle.

"You're the surfer I read about, aren't you?" George asked. "In the paper the other day?"

"Yes."

"You were in the paper?" Evan asked. "It wasn't about me injuring your arm, was it?"

"No. They did an article on my career."

"Why didn't you tell me? I want to read it."

"It's no big deal," Danielle said. "But Grandma does have a few copies." She laughed. "Maybe a dozen or so."

"That explains the sling," Betsy said. "What did Evan do to you?"

"It was an accident," Evan said.

Danielle laughed again. "Yes, it was. And it was partly my fault."

"Were you surfing?" George asked.

"I was giving Evan a lesson."

"Now it's even clearer," Betsy said.

Evan flapped his arms. "It was an accident."

Betsy nudged him with her elbow. "I'm just teasing you."

"How far have you guys gotten?" Evan asked.

"Forty-six laps," George said. "You?"

"We're on number thirty-eight."

"I can't believe this many people are doing this," Betsy said.

The track was filled with hundreds of people and passing slower walkers required a bit of weaving.

"Thanks to Evan," George said. He clamped a hand on Evan's shoulder. "I should hire you to work for me. Maybe we could increase our customer base."

"I don't think my brother would go for that. Besides, I could never leave HankMed."

"Don't blame you. Must be easier than banking."

"Plus," Betsy said, nudging George in the ribs, "if you had more customers I'd see even less of you."

"But think of the extra shopping you could do," George said.

"Hmm. Maybe I should rethink this," Betsy said.

Evan suddenly stopped.

"What is it?" Danielle asked.

"It's them," he said, pointing toward the row of booths across the track.

"Them who?" George asked, his gaze turning in the direction Evan pointed.

"That couple. Who've been selling drugs to kids." He grabbed Danielle's arm. "Let's go."

He half dragged Danielle across the track and the infield, but by the time they reached the row of booths the couple had disappeared.

"Where are they?" Danielle asked.

Evan looked each way. "I don't know. They were right here."

Then he saw them. A few booths down, walking away from them. "There." He started after them.

The stringy-haired woman glanced over her shoulder at Evan. She nudged the guy and he looked Evan's way, too. Evan pushed through the crowd, Danielle following.

The couple veered right and disappeared between two booths. Evan picked up his pace. He and Danielle cut between the two booths. Now they stood looking along the back of the row of booths. The couple was nowhere to be seen.

"You go that way," Evan said. "I'll go along the back."

Evan circled the entire row of booths, finally catching up with Danielle again near the far goalposts.

"Anything?" Danielle asked.

"No."

They made another lap around the booths but didn't see the couple. They gave up and rejoined the walk. Evan's head remained on a swivel, constantly checking the booths that flanked the track.

"They just disappeared," Evan said. "How does that happen?"

"It's a crowded place. Easy to hide."

"Not from Lawson, Evan R. Lawson."

Danielle laughed. "Even Bond, James Bond, lost Blofeld's trail from time to time."

"Bond was a hack compared to Evan R. Lawson."

Danielle laughed and hooked an arm with his. "Then let's finish this walk so you can get back on the case."

"I wish I had my spy cane with me."

"Why? You don't have any high-tech tracking devices in the secret compartment yet."

Evan shrugged. "Still, it would be cool."

"It'll be cool when we finish and get out of this heat."

They walked in silence for a couple of laps and then Evan noticed a man about a hundred feet ahead of them begin to stagger. To his left, his right, and then his knees buckled and he dropped to the track, facedown. Evan ran toward him. A crowd gathered as the walking procession came to a halt.

Evan knelt by the man, rolled him onto his back, and shook him. "Sir? Are you okay?"

The man groaned and took a deep breath.

Evan shook him again. "Can you hear me?"

"What?" The man's eyes were glassy and he didn't seem able to focus.

Evan looked up at Danielle. "Go get Hank."

She disappeared through the thickening crowd.

"Need some help?" It was Peggy Whitmire, the high school PE instructor. She knelt on the opposite side of the man.

"I don't know what happened," Evan said. "He was walking and then he collapsed."

Peggy reached for the man's neck, pressing her fingers in. "His pulse is fast and a little weak." Now she shook the man. "Can you hear me?"

The man's gaze finally found her. "What happened?"

"You fainted."

The man tried to sit up, but Peggy placed a palm on his chest. "Just lie here a minute."

Hank and Divya pushed their way through the crowd.

"Man, am I glad to see you," Evan said.

"What happened?"

"He collapsed," Evan said. "He was just in front of us. He sort of staggered and then fell."

"I called the medics," someone in the crowd said.

Evan watched as Hank gave him a quick exam, listening to his heart and lungs. Divya checked his blood pressure.

"One-ten over sixty. Pulse one hundred."

"Let's get him into the shade."

Just then the crowd parted to let the medic van roll up onto the track. Two medics jumped out.

"What have you got, Dr. Lawson?" one of them asked.

"Looks like he got a little overheated."

"Been seeing a bunch of that."

"Can you help us get him over to our booth?"

"Sure thing." He looked at his partner. "Let's load him up."

"Good job," Hank said.

"We didn't really do anything," Danielle said. "Except go get you."

"That's all you needed to do. Once we get some fluids in him I suspect he'll be fine."

Danielle laughed. "At least we were here instead of chasing that ghost couple."

"What ghost couple?" Hank asked.

"That couple I saw at the beach," Evan said. "The ones selling drugs."

"You saw them?"

"Yes, but we couldn't catch up to them. This is twice they've given me the slip."

"Ah, the life of a superspy," Hank said.

"Not feeling so super right now."

"Let's finish our laps, and then we'll go look for them again," Danielle said.

"How many more?" Hank asked.

"Eight," Danielle said. "Then we'll have reached our goal."

Back at the HankMed booth, Divya placed an oxygen mask on Michael Tobin and then while I started an IV, she hooked up the EKG machine. As we did this I asked him a dozen questions and found out he was fifty-three and in good health except for mild hypertension. He took a single blood pressure med but nothing else. He had been walking for two hours and hadn't often stopped for water.

"Pretty stupid, huh?" he said.

I shrugged. "Glad you said it so I wouldn't have to." I smiled.

"I know better."

"You're not alone," Divya said. "Most of what we've seen today has been problems with the heat."

"Thanks to you guys I'm feeling a lot better. I'm thirsty. Can I have something to drink?"

The liter bag of IV fluids I had hung was almost empty and his last BP reading was up to one-twenty over eighty.

"Sure."

While I helped him sit up, Divya grabbed a bottle of Wiggins lemon-lime and handed it to him. He gulped down half of it.

"Man, that's good." He looked at the label. "I've never had this before."

"Jonathan Wiggins makes it," I said. "He's got a booth just down the way."

Michael drained the bottle and Divya handed him another.

"I feel pretty good now," Michael said. "When can I get out of here?"

The IV bag was nearing empty. "Let's run the rest of this in, and then I'll take the IV out and you'll be good to go."

"Can I finish my walk?"

"Not sure I'd do that," I said.

"But I promised all my donors I'd do sixty laps. They're counting on me."

"Think of all the money you'll save them if you come up short," Divya said.

"I never thought of that." Michael laughed. "You could be right."

"How far have you gotten?" I asked.

"Forty-eight. Just twelve more to go. Three miles. That's all I need."

I shrugged.

"I'll go slow."

"And drink lots of fluids?" Divya said.

"When I leave here I'm heading down to Wiggins's booth. I promise."

"Okay, but take it slow and easy," I said. "If you feel anything unusual, any fatigue or light-headedness, stop and get back over here."

"Will do."

Chapter 22

Almost as soon as Michael Tobin left the booth a teen-age girl showed up. Obviously agitated, she rubbed her arms up and down. Her eyes were glazed, pupils dilated.

"What's the matter?" I asked.

"I don't know." Her gaze flitted around, seemingly unable to lock on to anything. "I feel like . . . I don't know."

"What's your name?"

She looked toward the ceiling, then out toward the infield, and then finally her gaze returned to me. "What?"

"Your name?"

"Uh . . . I . . . uh . . ." She looked panicked. She gave her head a shake as if trying to knock something loose. "Uh . . . Jessica. My name's Jessica Michaels."

"Sit down," I said.

I directed her to the exam table, where she sat on the

edge, one foot doing a tap dance in the air. Her lips and fingers trembled.

She pushed her shoulder-length brown hair back with both hands and shook her head. "What's wrong with me? Everything in my head is doing cartwheels."

"Cartwheels?" I asked.

Divya wrapped the blood pressure cuff around one arm and began inflating it.

She squeezed her head between her hands. "My thoughts. They seem to be tumbling all over each other. I can't stop them."

"BP's one-ninety over one hundred," Divya said as the BP cuffed hissed out its air.

"Lie down here," I said.

"I can't," Jessica said. "I have to move." She stood.

"Jessica, look at me," I said.

She tried.

"What did you take?"

"Nothing." She looked toward the entrance and started to move that way.

I grabbed her arm. She tried to pull away, but I held on.

"Call McCutcheon and Hyatt," I said to Divya and then to Jessica, "Listen to me. You need to stay here so we can help you."

"Help me? Help me do what?" She shook her head back and forth. "What's wrong with me? Am I going crazy?"

"No." I managed to get her settled on the exam table again. "You took something. What was it?"

"Nothing."

"Jessica, you have to tell me the truth so I can help you."

"Nothing. I didn't take anything."

"Let me guess," I said. "A harmless-looking little pink pill?"

"How'd you—" She caught herself. "I didn't take anything."

"Do I look stupid?" I asked. She stared at me but didn't respond, so I went on. "I know you took something and I think I know what. It's called Strawberry Quick. It's dangerous. It's scrambled your brain and that's what you're feeling."

McCutcheon showed up. "What's the problem?"

"I want you to meet Jessica," I said. "Jessica, this is Sergeant McCutcheon."

Jessica looked at him, her gaze traveling up and down, obviously taking in his tourist outfit. She looked even more confused than before.

"You called the cops?" she asked.

"You aren't the only one taking these drugs."

"But I didn't—"

"Jessica, give it a rest," I said. "When we get you over to the hospital and draw some blood we'll know what you took anyway."

"Hospital? I'm not going to any hospital." She jumped off the table but couldn't get by McCutcheon, who stood in her path, his massive arms crossed over his equally massive chest. "Let me by."

McCutcheon shook his head. "Not going to happen."

She whirled toward me. "You can't do this." Her gaze bounced around as if she was looking for an escape route. With McCutcheon blocking the front and Divya the back, she had nowhere to go. She began to cry, burying her face in her hands.

I wrapped an arm around her shoulder and helped her back onto the exam table. I let her cry it out for a couple of minutes.

"Jessica, the drug you took is methamphetamine with some ecstasy in it. That combination has caused you to react this way. Your tumbling thoughts. Your excitement and agitation and elevated blood pressure. We need to give you some meds to bring you down, but you'll need to be monitored in the hospital while we do."

She cried harder.

"Divya's going to give you something to settle this down and then we'll get the medics to take you over to Hamptons Heritage." I turned to Divya. "Ten milligrams of Thorazine."

Ten minutes later the injection began to take effect and Jessica settled back to earth. Her BP was down, her trembling had stopped, and she was much more coherent. She said the tumbling in her head was better. Not gone, but better.

Principal Hyatt arrived. Jill was with him. When I told them the story, Hyatt looked injured. As if he had personally failed.

"Jessica, you know better than this," Hyatt said. "You're one of our best students. A class leader. I didn't know you were involved in anything like this."

She sniffed back tears. "I'm not. I swear. I've never done anything like this before."

"Why now?"

She shook her head, her gaze dropping to her lap. "I don't know. Just something to try." She looked up at Hyatt. "All the other kids do, so I thought I'd see what the big deal was."

"Where'd you buy it?"

"I didn't. Someone gave it to me."

"Who?" McCutcheon asked.

She looked at him and then at Hyatt. "Just some dude."

"Jessica?" Hyatt said. "I know you. You didn't get some pill from some stranger and swallow it. You got it from someone you know. Someone you trust."

See what I mean? Doctors and high school principals get lied to all the time.

"He told me it was nothing." Her voice was soft, almost a mumble.

"Who?" Hyatt said.

"Do I have to say?"

"That depends. Do you want another of your classmates to go through what you're going through?"

"No." She sighed. "It was Billy. Billy Presley."

"I see."

"I take it you know this Billy?" McCutcheon asked.

"Yes. He's a junior. Like Jessica."

"Let's go find him," McCutcheon said. "If he's still here."

"No," Jessica said. "He'll know I told you."

"We won't let him know," Hyatt said.

"Where did you last see him?" Jill asked.

"Over by the refreshment stand. Maybe an hour ago. I don't know where he is now."

McCutcheon and Hyatt left.

The medics pulled up behind the booth and we settled Jessica on a stretcher for her trip to Hamptons Heritage. I had called her parents and they were headed to the hospital. Not happy, but that's the way it was.

"Pretty stupid, huh?" Jessica asked.

"Yeah," I said. "But the worst is behind you."

"You don't know my parents."

"Let me make a prediction. They'll be mad. Then they'll be scared, and then they'll be supportive. Just give it time."

"I hope you're right."

Things returned to normal after Jessica left. Divya and I saw a few bumps and scrapes and half a dozen dehydrated folks but nothing major. Until Patrick Knight and his mother, Rochelle, showed up again. Patrick was walking gingerly, one hand plastered to his left side.

Before I could ask what the problem was, Patrick said, "I won. Like I told you I would."

"The long jump?" I asked.

"And three races. The hundred, the two-twenty, and the four hundred."

"That's pretty good."

"It was too much, you ask me," Rochelle said. "I think he did some damage with that long jump."

"Like what?" I asked.

Rochelle nodded to Patrick. "Tell him."

"I think it's the flu," Patrick said.

"It's no flu," Rochelle said. "You did something to yourself with all that running around and jumping. Now you tell the doctor everything."

"Why do you think it's the flu?" I asked.

"'Cause I ache all over."

"Any cough or shortness of breath?"

"No. Just aching. But not like it usually is when I have a bug. My joints hurt. My belly, too."

"Let's take a look."

I had Patrick strip off his T-shirt and sit on the exam table. His lungs were clear, no palpable nodes in his neck, and his heart was normal. His abdomen was another story. I had him lie back and performed a complete abdominal examination. Very tender, particularly in the left upper quadrant. When I pressed my fingers into that area he withdrew and winced audibly.

"Sorry. How long has this been going on?"

"The joint pain began a couple of days ago and this whatever it is in my belly began yesterday."

"But you didn't tell anyone?"

"I just did."

I laughed. "But you didn't tell your mother, and you certainly didn't tell me yesterday."

"Because I had jumping and running to do. I'm all done now."

He tried to sit up, grunting in the process, but I held him back.

"Just lie there," I said.

"Man, that hurts." He pressed an open palm over his abdomen.

"Any nausea or vomiting or diarrhea?"

Patrick shook his head. "None of that."

"Have you ever had anything like this before?"

"Not really."

"Not really is not really no," I said with a smile.

He laughed, which apparently caused discomfort, since he now placed both hands over his belly and said, "I've got to remember not to do that."

"So you've had similar episodes in the past?"

"Not exactly. This is worse."

"Tell me about them. The ones you've had in the past."

"Sometimes when I get the flu or when I do too much running or other sports I'll get pains in my muscles and joints."

"How often does that happen?" I glanced at Rochelle.

"Don't ask me. He don't tell me nothing."

"If I did I'd never get to do anything."

"So, how often?" I asked again.

"I don't know. Sometimes."

"How long do the symptoms last when they happen?"

"A few hours. Sometimes a couple of days. They always go away." He glanced at Divya and then back at me. "But I've never had anything this bad."

"Did Patrick ever see a doctor about these other episodes?" Divya asked Rochelle.

Before she could answer, Patrick shook his head and his chin came up. "I'm not big on doctors." He glanced at me. "Sorry."

"That's okay. But we don't bite." Then I asked Rochelle, "Anyone in the family with similar problems?"

"Patrick's daddy," Rochelle said. "He complained of the same stuff sometimes. Aching joints and muscles. Mostly after he'd been drinking. 'Course I haven't seen or spoken with him for years. Maybe five years. Not since he took off to Miami."

"Anyone else?"

"Not that I know."

"Any disease in your family? Diabetes or anything like that?"

"My dad does have sickle cell, but it doesn't really bother him. As far as I know. I don't see him very often either."

"Sickle cell?" Divya said. "Has Patrick ever been tested for that?"

She shook her head. "You heard him. He don't like doctors. I'm amazed he agreed to come see you."

"Dr. Hank is cool," Patrick said. "And funny."

Coming from Patrick that was quite an endorsement. I was glad Evan wasn't here. He'd try to turn it into an ad campaign.

"I want to draw some blood," I said. "Then Divya will do an X-ray and ultrasound of your abdomen."

"I'm not going to no hospital," Patrick said.

"You don't have to. We can do them right here. Just take a minute to set it up."

"Cool."

I drew the blood and while Divya took the X-rays, I carried the blood sample out to the van, where I made slides, stained them, and looked at them through our digital microscope.

Bingo. The diagnosis jumped right out at me.

Sickle-cell anemia is an odd disease. It's genetic and tends to run in families of African origin. The defect is with the hemoglobin, the oxygen-carrying molecule in the red blood cells. It's abnormal in this disease and the abnormality causes the red blood cells to take on a sickle appearance. They look like little half-moons. That's exactly what I saw on Patrick's blood smear.

These abnormal cells might look like innocent little smiley faces under the microscope, but they can be extremely treacherous. Their shape causes them to snag and clump and pile up in small blood vessels, slowing or blocking blood flow. This can lead to joint and muscle pain. Red blood cells, as part of their normal life cycle, are filtered through the spleen. Sickle cells can sludge in the spleen's intricate network of blood vessels and cause damage, even a rupture, of this delicate organ.

That was what was going on with Patrick.

By the time I returned to the booth, Divya had completed the X-rays and the ultrasound and loaded the digital images onto her laptop. I examined them. Everything appeared normal except that the spleen was slightly enlarged.

I told Patrick and his mother what I had found on his blood smear.

"What does this mean?"

"That your grandfather, through your mother, and maybe your father, passed this along to you. That you inherited the same disease they have."

"That's what's causing all this pain?" Rochelle asked.

"Absolutely." I went on to explain what was happening inside Patrick's body. "The major problem here is the pain in your abdomen. The spleen is involved and that's a potentially dangerous situation."

"I don't like the sound of that," Patrick said.

"Remember earlier when I said you didn't have to go to the hospital?"

"Yeah."

"I lied."

His eyes widened.

"Not exactly lied, since I didn't know what we were dealing with then. Now I do. I'm afraid you'll have to get over to Hamptons Heritage."

"No way." Patrick looked at his mother. "Tell him I'm a quick healer. I can fix this at home."

"You sure the hospital is necessary?" Rochelle asked.

"I'm afraid so. The treatment for this is bed rest, IV fluids, and pain medications while we evaluate his spleen more thoroughly. It's possible that it might have to be removed."

"Are you talking about an operation?" Patrick said. "No way. I'm not going to have anyone cut on me."

"You might not have a choice. But let's not go too far

down that road until we get you over to Hamptons Heritage and see how everything goes."

"Come on, dude. Do I really have to?"

"Afraid so. Trust me, you don't want to deal with a ruptured spleen. If you think it hurts now wait until that happens. Not to mention it could kill you."

Patrick rolled his huge eyes. "I'm starting not to like you so much."

"Now my feelings are hurt."

"Not as much as my spleen, or whatever you call that thing in there."

Chapter 23

Divya and I watched the medics pull away and disappear through the exit gate.

"That young man is something else," Divya said.

"Twelve going on thirty-five. I get the feeling his mother is overmatched."

"True. But they seem to have a good relationship."

"Not to mention that Patrick seems focused on school and sports and not drugs like the other kids we've seen."

You know the old admonition that if you think something or, worse, say it out loud, it will happen? It's hocus-pocus to me, but some people believe it. Sort of like the movie *Beetlejuice*. If you said his name three times, he would appear and chaos would follow. Same thing here except that I mentioned kids and drugs once and three showed up.

Just like that.

As if I had summoned them or something.

The three teens—one boy, two girls—were hammered. No doubt. A diagnosis anyone could make from across the room. One, a girl with short black hair and glassy eyes, severely so. The other two were helping her into the booth.

"Are you the doctor?" the boy asked.

"I'm Dr. Lawson," I said as I helped the girl onto the exam table. "What's the matter?"

"I don't know," the other girl said. She had red hair, pale freckled skin, the beginnings of a sunburn on her exposed shoulders, and glazed blue eyes.

"What's your name?" I asked the girl sitting before me.

She stared back.

"It's Alaina," the boy said. "I'm Cory and this is my sister, Carrie," he said, indicating the redhead.

"What's the problem?" Divya asked. She began wrapping the blood pressure cuff around Alaina's arm. The girl sat quietly but watched Divya's every move as if she couldn't quite grasp what was happening.

"I don't know," Carrie said. "She's acting all weird."

"Weird?"

"You know. Like out of it. I mean like I'm not sure she knows who we are."

"What did she take?"

Carrie's gaze left mine and jumped to her brother as if hoping he had an answer. He obviously didn't.

"Nothing," Carrie said.

"BP is one-fifty over one hundred. Pulse one-thirty-five," Divya said.

My exam showed that Alaina had dilated pupils that were poorly reactive and hyperactive reflexes. Just like the other kids we had seen.

I turned to the brother and sister team. "'Nothing' isn't going to work here. What did you guys take?"

They looked at each other but said nothing.

"Alaina is intoxicated. We're going to send her over to Hamptons Heritage."

"No—," Carrie began.

I stopped her by extending my palm toward her. "Yes. And once she's there they'll draw some blood, test it, and we'll know what she took. But the sooner we know, the quicker we can help her. She could be in danger. Her blood pressure is high and her heart is galloping. So, what did you guys take?"

Both stared at the floor.

"Do you want something really bad to happen to her?"

Now they looked at me and then each other, but neither said a word.

What is with these kids? Not just these three, but the ones we had seen over the past two days. Even Kevin Moxley. Okay, I understand not confessing your sins, but these two were worried enough to drag Alaina in here, fear etched on their faces, yet they refused to talk.

"Really? That's it? You bring her here and then refuse to tell me what's going on?"

Cory shoved his hands into the pockets of his shorts and rolled one sneaker up on its side, but that's all I got.

"She's your friend. Right?"

Nothing. I did notice Carrie's lower lip tremble.

"I'll ask again . . ."

From the edge of my visual field I saw Alaina sway. I turned just as her eyes rolled back and she went limp, falling forward. I managed to grab her, her head lolling against my shoulder. I laid her back on the exam table and checked her carotid pulses. Very fast, very faint.

"Alaina?" I shook her shoulders.

No response. Divya began hooking up our portable cardiac monitor while I listened to her lungs. At least she was still breathing, even if in a shallow and erratic manner.

The monitor popped to life as Divya fastened the final lead into place.

"V-tach," I said. "One hundred milligrams of Lidocaine."

While Divya drew the Lido into a syringe, I started an IV, frequently monitoring Alaina's wrist pulse in the process. If she lost her pulse or stopped breathing, we'd have to begin CPR.

As I taped the IV into place, I looked at Cory. He and his sister were wide-eyed and openmouthed as they watched.

"See the medics over there?" I asked Cory.

He stared at Alaina, unmoving, as if he hadn't heard me.

"Cory, look at me." He did. "The medics are directly across from us. Run over there and tell them to get over here." He stood as if embedded in the ground. "Cory, do it now."

That seemed to snap him back to reality. He turned and ran a straight line toward the medic station.

"Here you go," Divya said, handing me the syringe.

I injected the Lido and waited a minute, watching the monitor. No change in her rhythm.

"Let's hook up the defibrillator."

While Divya attached the defib patches, I drew up another hundred milligrams of Lido and gave it. Her V-tach ignored it and stubbornly remained at a rate of around one-ninety.

"Okay," I said, "let's zap her. We'll start with two hundred watt-seconds."

Divya hit the CHARGE button and the defibrillator whined as its capacitor charged. Once it finished, Divya said, "Ready."

"Do it."

"Clear," Divya said and then pressed the red button, delivering the charge.

Alaina twitched, recoiled, and moaned. The charge spiked the EKG monitor for a second and then her rhythm reappeared. "Sinus tachycardia about one-ten."

"Good. It worked."

Alaina began to come around, trying to talk and sit up. This confused state after a period of very low blood pressure and after an electric shock is not unusual. I held her down.

"Alaina?" I said.

Her eyes fluttered open but didn't focus.

"Alaina?" I repeated.

Her gaze landed on me and her eyes fought to focus. She appeared confused and disoriented.

"Don't move. You're okay."

The medic van pulled up, followed by Cory, who was gasping from his run back and forth across the field. Two medics climbed out.

It took a few minutes for me to explain to them what had happened, after which they loaded Alaina into the back and drove away, lights flashing, siren attracting attention and moving people out of the way.

I returned my attention to Cory and Carrie. Both appeared pale, eyes still wide.

"Do you know Alaina's home number?"

"I do," Carrie said. She rattled off the number.

Divya flipped open her cell and dialed the number. While she told Alaina's mother what had happened and that her daughter was on the way to Hamptons Heritage, I leaned on Cory and Carrie.

"See what I mean by something bad happening?"

"What was that?" Cory asked. "What happened to her?"

"The drug she took made her heart go haywire. Nearly killed her. If she hadn't been here it probably would have."

I saw tears collect in Carrie's eyes.

"So, I'll ask again . . . where did you get the drugs?"

"They're not drugs," Carrie said. "Not really. They're just harmless natural pills."

"Did what just happened with Alaina seem harmless or natural to you?"

"No."

"Let me take a wild guess," I said. "Someone here sold you some pretty pink pills. You each took one and at first it seemed cool. Fun. But then Alaina got freaky and you freaked out. Close?"

Cory nodded.

"See, that was easy."

"She actually took three of them," Cory said and then glanced at his sister. "We only took one, but Alaina took three. We told her not to."

"Who'd you buy them from?"

"Some random dude," Cory said.

"Someone you don't know? Never seen before?"

"That's right. Some guy we don't know."

He would have been convincing except that his gaze kept dropping toward the ground and a small twitch appeared at the corner of his left eye.

"Hank?"

I looked up. It was Jill. Behind her stood McCutcheon, Hyatt, and a guy who I assumed was Billy Presley. A thin, wiry kid with shaggy hair, blue shorts, an oversized white T-shirt, and eyes dilated with fear. And maybe drugs. Probably the stuff he was selling.

Cory's entire demeanor changed. His eyes widened and then he began looking around as if searching for an escape route.

Bingo.

"Is that the guy you don't know?" I said. "The random dude?"

McCutcheon stepped forward. "What's going on?"

"Three more customers, I think. Unfortunately one of them nearly died and is now on the way to Hamptons Heritage."

Billy's eyes jerked wide open and he started to say something, but McCutcheon rested a hand on his shoulder and gave it a squeeze. Billy got the hint and fell silent. McCutcheon then looked down at Cory. "I'm Sergeant McCutcheon. Did you buy drugs from Billy here?" Cory hesitated. "You do understand that lying to a police officer is serious business, don't you?"

Cory nodded.

"Yes," Carrie said. "We got them from Billy."

All eyes turned toward Billy, who now had that deer-in-the-headlights look.

McCutcheon nodded. "Seems Billy's been selling for our mysterious couple. That's why we haven't seen them around."

"Actually," I said, "Evan saw them a little while ago. Over among the booths on the other side. He tried to follow them, but they slipped away."

"So they're still here somewhere," McCutcheon said, more a statement than a question.

"They were then. Who knows about now. Evan might have spooked them."

"Their van is in the lot. They aren't," McCutcheon said. "I've got a couple of guys watching it."

"Maybe they'll return to it," I said.

"Maybe. We were thinking they might have abandoned it. Maybe found out we were here undercover and split. Afraid to go back to the van. But if Evan saw them maybe they're still around. Maybe they'll get stupid and we'll get lucky."

"Is that where you picked up the pills?" I asked Billy. "At the van?"

He nodded.

"When?"

"A couple of hours ago."

"Do you know them?" I asked.

"Not really."

"Just enough to do their dirty work? Is that it?"

He shrugged.

"Names? Do you know their names?"

"All I know is Pete and Erin." He glanced up at McCutcheon. "I swear that's all I know."

"Have you sold for them before?" I asked.

He shook his head.

"Just today?"

He nodded.

"How'd they pick you?"

He stared at me.

"I mean, there are a lot of high school kids around here. Why'd they pick you?"

"I bought some stuff from them. Earlier today. I gave some to a friend of mine."

"That would be Jessica Michaels," McCutcheon said.

I nodded. "She's pretty messed up. And she's in the hospital."

"What?" Billy said. "The hospital? Her, too?"

"You see, Billy," I said, "that makes two people this

stuff you're passing around has harmed enough that they require a visit to the hospital."

Tears gathered in Billy's eyes. "They said it was safe. Just fun."

"It's not. So again, why did they pick you?"

"When I went back to their van and asked for some more they jacked the price. From five dollars a pill to ten. I told them I couldn't pay that, so they said there was a way I could earn some for free."

"Sell it to your friends?"

He nodded. "I didn't know."

"How many did you sell?"

"A couple of dozen."

"Pills or people?" I asked.

"People. Maybe twice or three times that many pills. Most wanted two or three."

"And when you ran low you what? Went back by the van and got some more?"

"And gave them the money."

"And they paid you?"

"With pills. For every five I sold they gave me one to sell or use myself." He kicked at the ground. "I sold them all."

"When did you see them at the van last?"

"An hour or more ago. The last time I went by it was locked up and they weren't there."

"Van's registered to a Peter Anders," McCutcheon said. "We got the word out. Already had someone knock on his door. Not home. But we know who we're looking for now, so it's just a matter of time."

The time in question turned out to be about thirty seconds.

Evan R. Lawson, superspy, to the rescue.

My cell rang, and when I answered Evan was jabbering a mile a minute, his voice just above a whisper.

"Whoa, slow down."

He tried. Not easy for Evan when he's revved up. "They're here. I'm looking right at them."

"Where?"

McCutcheon's eyebrows raised.

"The parking area behind the school gym."

"What are they doing?"

"She's digging around in a black canvas bag and he's talking on his cell phone." I heard a noise. "Just a sec." His voice was lower. "I thought he might have seen us, but I don't think so."

"Us?"

"Danielle's with me. The dude's all totally spooked about something. Keeps looking around."

"Where are you?"

"Hiding in some shrubbery. Maybe two hundred feet from them."

"Don't move and don't do anything stupid. We're on the way." I closed my phone and looked at McCutcheon. "Behind the gym. Evan and Danielle are there."

I was out of the booth before McCutcheon could take a step. As I ran toward the school, McCutcheon was with me, talking into his radio. He told all his guys to head toward the gym and to call for backup.

We found Evan and Danielle at the same time Officer Tommy Griffin found us. We all huddled behind the shrubbery.

"I have two units rolling this way," Griffin said.

McCutcheon nodded. "Let's do it."

McCutcheon told us to stay put, and he and Griffin pushed through the row of shrubs and walked toward the couple. At first the couple didn't see them coming, but then the Pete dude turned and froze as if his feet had melted to the asphalt. Now Erin looked up and she, too, froze.

"Peter Anders?" McCutcheon said. "Keep your hands where I can see them."

Three of the undercover guys showed up. They easily handcuffed the couple. Both Pete and Erin appeared too shocked to resist.

"She threw something in the Dumpster," Evan shouted. "The one on the left."

McCutcheon turned and looked at us and then nodded toward the three Dumpsters that sat against the side wall of the gym.

Two of the officers opened the bin Evan had indicated. One vaulted inside and began rummaging through the debris. In half a minute he held up two plastic zip bags, gripping them by their corners. Each brimmed with bright pink pills.

"Those aren't mine," Pete said.

"So we won't find your fingerprints on the bags, then. Right?" McCutcheon asked.

A car sped around the corner of the gym and into

the lot. It came to a sudden stop, hesitated a minute, and then the rear wheels spun as the driver reversed his course. He swung the car around, obviously intending to retrace his path. Didn't work. Two patrol cars cut him off.

This one was easy to figure. Somehow Pete and Erin had discovered that the cops were on to them. They abandoned their van, tried to dump the pills, and called a friend, or maybe a fellow dealer, to whisk them away.

Only took a few minutes to bag up the evidence, arrest the two guys driving the car, and settle Pete and Erin into a patrol car. McCutcheon spoke with his guys briefly and then everyone dispersed, the patrol cars heading toward the police station.

We headed back toward the HankMed booth.

"Good job," McCutcheon said to Evan.

In a flash Evan had his cell phone out.

Evan R. Lawson is a superspy.

"What's that?" McCutcheon asked.

"You don't want to know," I said.

McCutcheon actually smiled and then nodded as if he understood. Maybe he had a goofy brother, too.

"I need to head to the station," McCutcheon said. "And have a chat with our drug-dealing couple."

"That should be interesting," I said.

He shrugged. "Maybe. Probably not. They'll lie and I'll lean on them. They'll try to blame someone else, but I'll cut off all those avenues. Finally they'll confess and I'll pass everything along to the DA."

"Sounds like you've done this before," I said.

"Too often. But nine times out of ten that's more or less how it goes." He nodded. "Thanks for your help in all this."

We shook hands. He congratulated Danielle and Evan again for their good work and then he left.

Evan, Danielle, and I walked back to the HankMed booth. Cory and Carrie weren't there, so I asked Divya where they were.

"Their mother was here at the fair. She brought them. And Alaina. When she couldn't find them she came by. Worried that something had happened."

"Something did."

Divya nodded. "True. Just not what she expected. When I told her what had happened to Alaina, she was at first scared and then she was furious."

"Can't say I blame her."

"They're on the way to the hospital to see Alaina and her mother."

"Wouldn't want to be Carrie or Cory," Evan said.

"Or Alaina," Danielle added.

Chapter 24

I picked Jill up for the dinner I'd promised her. She looked hot. Little black dress and all. I told her so.

"You look nice, too, Dr. Lawson," she said.

I did. I wore my best blue suit, white shirt, and red tie. I'm not big on suits and ties, but this was a special occasion.

"I even washed behind my ears," I said.

"That's good to know." She brushed a bit of lint from my jacket sleeve. "You should dress up more often."

"It might hurt my reputation."

"True." She laughed. "But you look okay in jeans, too."

"As do you, Ms. Casey."

"You don't have to take me to dinner," she said.

"Really? I thought I did."

"It's not a real date."

"It's not? After I washed my ears and wore a suit?"

"But you didn't bring flowers."

I snapped my fingers. "I knew I forgot something."

She laughed. "No problem. I didn't really expect any."

"So you have low expectations."

"With you? I'd say yes."

"My feelings are hurt."

"Right. But I'd bet you could've talked Evan into cooking. He's on that jag now."

"I wouldn't want him around gas and sharp instruments tonight."

"Why?"

"He's manic. He cracked the big case. If you listen to him he deserves the Medal of Honor."

"He did find the bad guys."

"Yes, he did. But what would you expect from Evan R. Lawson, superspy?"

We both laughed.

Truth was that I was proud of my brother. He did track down the bad guys. He did crack the big drug case.

My brother the DEA agent.

"Or I could have cooked," Jill said. "Maybe not as fancy as Evan, but I know a couple of dishes you like."

"But this is your night, not mine."

She twisted slightly in her seat. "And why would this be my night?"

"You've worked hard the past few months on the fair. Particularly the last two days. You deserve a little fine dining and fine wine."

"So we're going for fine."

"Would you expect anything less from me?"

"A lot less."

"We could find a drive-through."

"Not in this dress."

"Then I guess we'll have to settle for fine."

"Where are we going?"

"Stella's."

"That is fancy. And very French."

"As I said, fine dining and fine wine."

"This isn't dutch, is it?"

I laughed. "No. This is on HankMed."

"So I'm a tax deduction?"

"Something like that."

"How romantic."

"I thought so, too."

Stella's was in East Hampton. It looked like a French country house. White with dark green trim and shutters and ivy framing the entrance. Inside it was quiet and elegant. Soft jazz from the piano player ensconced in one corner of the main dining room set the tone. The air was rich with the aroma of French sauces.

"Can I help you?" The attractive young woman stood behind the reception podium.

"Lawson party."

"Oh, yes. You must be Dr. Lawson." She smiled at me and then looked at Jill and nodded slightly. "Ms. Casey. Welcome to Stella's."

"Smells wonderful," I said.

"It tastes even better," she said. "Please, follow me."

As she led us through the main dining room, Jill grabbed my arm and whispered, "How'd she know who I was?"

"I must have told her."

We continued through the main room and down a short, narrow hallway.

"Hank Lawson, what are you up to?" Jill asked.

"Nothing."

"Here we are," the hostess said. She pushed open the door to a private dining room and we entered.

Inside, a group of friends awaited us. Evan and Divya, of course. Danielle and Angela Delaney, George and Betsy Shanahan, Marcy and Stephanie from Marcy's Bodyworks, and Principal Jerry Hyatt.

"Surprise!" they all shouted in unison.

Jill stood speechless for a minute and then looked at me. "I take it this is your doing."

I gave a half bow. "And Evan and Divya."

Tears collected in her eyes and she melted into the crowd, hugs and kisses following.

While Jill received her well-deserved accolades, I chatted with Danielle and Angela. A waiter brought me a glass of champagne and refilled Danielle's and Angela's glasses. Danielle was out of her sling and Angela had discarded her walker for a cane.

"My shoulder feels much better," Danielle said. "And before you ask, yes, I've been doing all my strength and range-of-motion exercises."

"No pain?" I asked.

"Very little. Just a little stiffness."

"It'll get better week by week."

She nodded. "I think I'll make that meet after all."

"How's your hip?" I asked Angela.

"You're not here to talk shop. You're here to celebrate Jill."

"True. I just can't help myself." I smiled.

She laughed. "I'm fine. Hated that walker, but I love this cane." She held it up. It was stained oak with a nonskid rubber tip and a faceted brass knob. "And if anybody tries to bother me I can brain them with it."

"Grandma," Danielle said.

"Well, I could."

"I don't think you'll have to," I said.

The clinking of a knife against a glass caught my attention. Everyone else's, too. It was Evan.

"Let's all take our seats," he said.

My brother, the master of ceremonies.

Everyone settled around the large oval table. I sat beside Jill.

Waiters appeared and began pouring wine. Orders were taken and conversations moved around and back and forth across the table.

"I can't believe you kept this from me," Jill said. "How long have you been planning this?"

"For about a month."

"And you kept it secret? Or a better question is, Evan kept it secret?"

"Evan kept what secret?" Evan asked.

"This," Jill said.

"Under threat of bodily harm," Evan said. "By Divya."

"Actually, this was Divya's idea," I said.

Divya sat across from us. She lifted her glass to Jill.

"Well, thank you. It's a very pleasant surprise."

I stood. Everyone looked at me. "Before dinner I want to make a toast." Everyone picked up a glass. "To Jill. For an incredible job with the First Annual Hamptons Health and Fitness Fair." I raised my glass. "I'm sure there will be many more."

Glasses pinged against one another and everyone toasted Jill.

"It was nothing," Jill said. "Only three months of my life."

That drew a round of laughter.

"I'd like to make another toast," Principal Hyatt said. "To Evan. For cracking the drug ring."

More pinging as Evan stood and bowed. His cell phone appeared.

Evan R. Lawson is a superspy.

My brother, Mr. Modest.

Dinner came and the conversation level declined as everyone dug in. I had ordered *poulet sauté* and Jill *blanquette de veau*. We shared and both were marvelous. For desert we each had Strawberries Romanoff. Wow.

After dinner we gathered in the bar for a nightcap. I sat next to Hyatt.

He leaned over, propping an elbow on the arm of his chair. "Before I came over I stopped by and saw Sergeant McCutcheon. He said his department had had twenty-three encounters. His word."

"Twenty-three?"

"Let me see if I remember correctly." He looked toward the ceiling as if recalling McCutcheon's words. "Two intoxicated teens at the beach, six in local ERs, four of those at Hamptons Heritage, and those at the health fair. The rest were either on the streets or driving."

"Makes you feel safe to be on the road, doesn't it?" I said.

"I thought about that as I drove over. I also thought about what I'm going to do next school year."

"And that would be?"

"We—by that I mean the school board and the education department—have always focused on the high schools." He shrugged. "Figuring that's where the major problem was. Seemed logical. Now I'm not so sure. Three of the kids that the police picked up were twelve." He sighed. "Can you imagine? Twelve?"

I started to say yes I could, but I let it go.

"I'm thinking we need to begin programs in middle school," Hyatt continued. "Even in grammar school."

"I'm afraid you're right."

"I just don't understand it. I don't know how it was when you were in school, but for me the worst thing any of my classmates did was beer and the occasional theft of their parents' harder stuff."

"Same for me. With a little marijuana tossed in. But those were few. I can still name the stoners in my school."

"And now we have this." He massaged the back of his neck. "Maybe I'm getting too old. Too far behind the times."

"I don't believe that. It's people like you that can turn this around."

"Can I? I don't know."

"Trying is all you can do."

"I suppose you're right."

A waitress appeared and asked if we needed anything. We both opted for mineral water and lime.

"This stuff is pretty bad, isn't it?" Hyatt asked.

"Yes, it is. Not the worst thing I've ever seen. I think PCP holds that honor. But this is a dangerous combination."

"And according to McCutcheon we've seen just a small slice of it."

"Oh?"

"He talked to a friend with the DEA. Apparently there are secret labs making this stuff from coast to coast. Every time one gets busted five more crop up." He sighed again. "I thought video games and the Internet were stealing our kids' souls. Seems petty by comparison."

"Did he say where these came from? Were they made locally?"

"His DEA guy said they probably came out of Queens. They've busted a few labs up there. Or maybe down near Brighton Beach." He stared at his shoes. "Truth is, they just aren't sure."

That depressing conversation took us to eleven o'clock. People began saying their good-byes, Danielle and Angela first. Evan had driven them, so he left with them. Marcy, Stephanie, and the Shanahans soon followed. Finally Jill, Divya, and I walked Hyatt out to his car. We stood and watched as he drove away.

"I wouldn't want his job," I said.

"I'm sure he says the same about yours," Divya said.

Chapter 25

I got lucky last night. Jill invited me to stay over. Our relationship had been off and on lately. Mostly off. Not that we were fighting or arguing about anything, just that we had opted for less entanglement. But I guess last night proved we needed a little together time. I know I did.

I awoke early. Jill was still asleep. I lay there and stared at the ceiling, going over everything that had happened in the past few days. I thought about this new and nasty drug that had popped up. About all the good kids we had seen. Kids who made some bad choices. Fortunately there had been no deaths, none that I was aware of anyway, so there was that. Still, this drug was out there and we would see more before long.

Some things in life are certain.

By the time Jill began to stir, my thoughts had traveled to Patrick Knight. One thing I knew about him was that he would be successful regardless of what he decided to do when he grew up. Smart, witty, and with a confident attitude that would take him far. Despite being from a broken home and now fighting a tough disease, Patrick would be okay. No doubt.

Even some good things were certain. That was comforting.

Jill yawned and stretched, then rolled on her side, looking at me.

"You're awake."

"I am."

"And you've just been lying there?"

"Thinking."

"About what?"

"You."

"Liar."

I rolled toward her. "No, I have been. And a few other things."

"Glad I was in there somewhere. What time is it?"

I looked past her at the clock radio that sat on the bedside table. "If that thing's right it's seven fifteen."

"Tell me I don't have to get up."

"You don't have to get up."

"But I'm hungry."

"I'll make you something."

"That'll be hard to do with an empty fridge."

"I'll go get bagels and coffee."

She yawned again. "No. I'll get up." She rolled out of bed. "Then you can take me for coffee and bagels."

That's what I did.

Before we left Jill's I called Evan and Divya and they met us at Frankie's Café. It was busy for a Fourth of

July morning—I expected most people to either be heading out for the beaches or prepping for an afternoon barbecue—but Frankie's was packed. Luckily we found a table near the back wall.

"Hmm, I'm hungry all of a sudden," I said.

"Couldn't imagine why," Jill said with a mischievous grin.

I had French toast, Jill a ham and cheese omelet. We shared. How cute.

"What time tonight?" Divya asked after finishing her bagel. "For the party before the party?"

Evan had decided to throw a small party at Shadow Pond so we could all get together before heading to Nathan's party.

"Six," Evan said. "I'm going to pick up Danielle and Angela about five thirty so we'll be back by then."

"Sure I can't bring anything?"

"Got it covered. It'll be basic. Champagne, wine, and a couple of tapas."

"Tapas?" I asked. "That's so colonial."

"The Spanish got here before the British," Evan said. "Besides, tapas are cool."

"I thought tapas were spicy."

"They are. And cool. You'll see."

After breakfast, Divya and I went to see a few follow-ups. Our first stop was to see Kevin Moxley. He was fine. In fact he was great. Still embarrassed by what he had done. "Stupid as a rock," is how he put it. I couldn't have agreed more.

Next we drove up to Sag Harbor to see Felicia Hecht. She felt great. After she began the new medicine, her headaches had disappeared.

"Now that they're gone," she said, "I realize how long they'd been going on. Maybe two years. But until they got bad I thought it was just fatigue or something like that. I feel better than I have in years."

I love it when things work out. When what you do makes a difference. It's that more than anything else that brings people into the medical profession. It was definitely what attracted me. So much of life simply goes along. Regardless of what you do, things are as they are. But to actually do something that helps? That's special.

"That was a good pickup," Divya said as we drove from Sag Harbor toward Hamptons Heritage. "Glossopharyngeal neuralgia. I'd never heard of it."

"Don't feel bad. Most docs haven't either, and even if they have they'll go their entire careers without ever seeing a case. I had. In med school. So I recognized it." I laughed. "Not initially, though. Like you, I thought she had an odd migraine syndrome."

At Hamptons Heritage, we found Patrick Knight in the ICU. Post-op. Apparently his spleen had begun leaking during the night and he had gone to surgery, returning to the ICU less one spleen.

Patrick's bed was cranked up to a half-sitting position. A broad bandage wrapped his abdomen. He looked up and gave us a groggy smile. He had that sleepy, euphoric look that comes only with post-op pain meds. His mother, Rochelle, sat in a chair next to him, thumbing through a magazine.

"How's it going?" I asked.

"He's driving the nurses crazy," Rochelle said. "He wants to eat and they won't let him."

"Not for a day or two," I said.

"But I'm hungry."

"That's a good sign," Divya said. "But you can't eat until your bowels wake up."

"They're awake," Patrick said. "I can hear them."

I laughed. "Good. Other than being hungry, how's everything else?"

"It hurts," Patrick said.

"It'll get better."

"It ain't much."

"Isn't," Rochelle said. "It isn't much."

Patrick rolled his eyes. "We ain't in school."

Rochelle scowled at him. "You're in my school. And don't be a smarty. They operated on your tummy, not your butt. I can still whack that."

"She didn't sleep much last night," Patrick said. "Makes her cranky."

"She's right, though," Divya said. "Good grammar lets people know how smart you are."

"People already know I'm smart," Patrick said.

"And modest," I said.

"That, too."

I looked through his chart. Vital signs normal, as were his morning labs. The op note showed he had lost very little blood during the surgery. I closed the chart and laid it on the edge of his bed. I then examined him. All was well and he even had bowel sounds. Those usually disappear after abdominal surgery for a day or two. In most people anyway. Patrick wasn't most people, though.

I had the feeling that he would sail through this with no problems. Except that of holding him down long enough for Mother Nature to do her healing. Somehow I didn't see Patrick slowing down for anyone or anything. A major surgery? A small bump in the road for him.

"Everything looks good," I said.

"When can I go home?"

See what I mean?

Rochelle shook her head. "You haven't even been out of bed yet. How can you talk about going home?"

"I got things to do. I can't lie around here."

"Slow down," I said. "It takes time to heal from something like this."

"How long?"

"Completely? A few weeks."

"Man, that sucks."

"Patrick," Rochelle said. "Don't you talk like that."

"Well, it does."

I laughed. "When you can get up and walk to the front door you'll be ready to go home."

"Well, let's go." He started to sit up but suddenly stopped and grabbed his belly. "Ouch."

"See?" I said. "Don't push it. A tough guy like you will be back to normal before you know it."

He dropped back against the pillow. "I don't have time for this."

Chapter 26

Evan was in full colonial spy mode. He twirled around the living room and then made Danielle do the same. Angela sat on the sofa, glass of champagne in her hand, laughing and encouraging their silliness. Her silver hair was twisted into a bun, and she wore a cobalt blue colonial ball gown and a sapphire necklace that she said was a family heirloom passed from her grandmother to her mother and then on to her. She looked outstanding.

Jill looked hot in her black and white Martha Washington dress and I was warming to my frontiersman outfit, fringe and all. Divya was gorgeous in her rose-colored colonial ball gown. The three of us watched Evan's and Danielle's antics from the safety of the kitchen. Best to stay away from the flying capes. Besides, the kitchen was where the food was and I was hungry, not having eaten since breakfast.

Evan had made an assortment of tapas: olives and

peppers in oil, *carne mechada*, pickled calamari rings with cilantro, chorizo in a wine sauce, and empanadas.

"These are great," Jill said as she took a bite of an empanada. "Where did you learn to make these?"

"Evan R. Lawson, master chef."

Good grief.

"It all works," Jill said. "I don't know which of these I like best."

"There's plenty," Evan said. "And I can always make some more."

Jill took another bite. "You might have to. They're addicting."

"Maybe you should have gone as a chef and not a spy," Divya said.

"But I am a spy. You said so yourself."

No, not the cell phone.

Evan R. Lawson is a superspy.

Too late.

Divya eyed the olive she held and then nodded toward Evan's cane. "You didn't accidentally get any of your spy poison on these, did you?"

"Only that one."

Divya raised an eyebrow. "What exactly do you have inside the secret compartment?"

Evan unscrewed the pear-shaped brass handle and angled the cane. He shook it and a shiny black tube slid out. He held it up.

"What's that?" Jill asked.

"My lipstick," Danielle said. She slid onto one of the counter stools.

Divya laughed. "What? A superspy with lipstick? No secreted poisons or weapons or battle plans?"

Evan's shoulders drooped. "I couldn't think of anything to put in there."

"And I don't have any pockets," Danielle said.

Divya had him right where she wanted him. I knew she was gearing up to fire for effect. She crossed her arms and arched one eyebrow. "Maybe you should have dressed as a makeup artist?"

Evan glared at her but offered no response.

"That would also be so Pimpernel."

"Are we back to that again?" Evan asked.

"I wasn't aware we'd ever left it," Divya said.

"Did they have makeup artists in colonial times?" I asked.

"Someone had to powder the wigs," Angela said.

Everyone laughed.

"Good one," Divya said. "Wish I had thought of it."

Jill and Divya carried the food trays over to the coffee table. Everyone followed, settling in the chairs that surrounded it. Danielle sat next to Angela on the sofa.

"Want something else, Grandma?" Danielle asked Angela.

"I shouldn't, but maybe some more of that marvelous calamari."

Danielle served up some on a small plate and handed it to her.

"I shouldn't. I've had too much already." She took a bite. "Evan, you outdid yourself with these. They are so good."

"And simple to make," Evan said.

"That's Evan," Divya said. "Simple to the core."

"A life lesson for all you youngsters," Angela said. "Never insult the chef."

I nodded. "Good advice."

Angela looked at Evan. "You know, with your cape and cane you could be a magician. Or maybe a sorcerer."

"I like that," Evan said. "A colonial sorcerer."

"Like Merlin?" I asked.

"Yeah," Evan said, getting into the idea now. "But I'd need one of those cool metal skullcaps like he wore in that movie."

"Maybe that would block the alien rays," Divya said.

"What alien rays?"

"The ones that are damaging the wiring in your brain."

Evan jutted his chin at her. "Maybe you should be a . . . a uh . . . a uh . . ."

"See what I mean?"

"Don't pick on Evan." Angela said.

"But you do have to admit that he is an attractive target," Divya said.

True.

The conversation turned to the health fair and Angela asked if Divya and I had been busy at our booth.

"Mainly people getting overheated and minor bumps and bruises," I said.

"And kids on drugs," Divya said.

"And don't forget Patrick Knight," Jill added.

"I stopped by Hamptons Heritage and saw him this morning," I said. "He's doing great."

"Did you say they took out his spleen?" Evan asked.

I nodded. I also noticed that Evan was rubbing his belly.

"Can you catch it?" Evan asked. "This sickle cell thing?"

"No. It's inherited."

"Are you sure?"

"I'm sure."

"But what if you're wrong?"

"He's not," Divya said.

"But my spleen hurts."

"No, it doesn't," I said.

"You don't know what my spleen feels like."

"You don't either."

"Sure I do. It hurts."

"Where?" I asked.

"Where what?"

"Where is your spleen?"

"Same place yours is."

"And where exactly is that?"

Evan didn't have an answer for that one.

Chapter 27

"Wow," Evan said. "Is this impressive or what?"

Evan's splenic troubles had apparently resolved and been replaced with overt awe at the transformation of Nathan Zimmer's mansion. He took it all in, eyes wide, jaw slack. Danielle and Angela, equally slack-jawed and wide-eyed, stood next to him.

"I've never seen anything like this," Angela said. "It's breathtaking."

Jill's fingers dug into my arm. "Can you believe this?"

I couldn't.

When we had seen it a few days ago, the day Jimmy Sutter decided to dissect his aorta, it was in transition. Now, the metamorphosis of Nathan's great room was complete, and as he had hoped, it did indeed look like an early American inauguration. Billowy red, white, and blue striped drapes covered three of the thirty-foot walls; the fourth, a bank of windows that opened onto the gardens and the ocean, was uncovered, allowing the soft twilight to bathe the room. The drapes were crowned with similar fabric, swagged between two-foot-high oval ceramic presidential portraits. Washington, Jefferson, Adams, and Madison faced us from across the room.

Two massive crystal chandeliers had been hung from the central beam. Adding more atmosphere than light, they looked like clusters of diamonds, or maybe stars and galaxies, against the dark ceiling.

A string quartet played music in one corner, but it was muted by the buzz of conversation. Waiters in frilly white shirts, gold-trimmed navy blue waistcoats, and powdered wigs, and waitresses in black and white Pilgrim costumes moved through the crowd with trays of food and champagne.

Nathan had spared no expense. Not that I'd thought he would.

Neither had the Hamptons crowd. The costumes were expensive and perfect. As if this was a Hollywood set and not a private party.

I saw ball gowns of every color, military uniforms, judges in black robes and powdered wigs, a couple of Ben Franklins, and red, white, and blue Betsy Ross costumes, white bonnets, tricorn and stovepipe hats, and three Pocahontas outfits.

A pair of waitresses approached us with silver trays filled with crystal champagne flutes. We each took a glass. A waiter appeared with a tray of shrimp and lobster bites. Everyone took a couple of pieces,

Evan tucking his cane beneath one arm so he could load a plate.

"So much for spies being quick and nimble," Divya said.

"You ate at the house. I didn't. I'm starving."

"You made all that stuff and then didn't eat any?" Danielle asked.

"I was too excited."

"About Danielle?" Angela asked. She raised an eyebrow.

"No. The party."

Angela shook her head. "I was trying to help you out, Evan."

"Oh. Sorry." He looked at Danielle. "I'm excited about being here with you, too."

"Too late," she said.

"Come on," Evan said. "You know what I mean."

Danielle punched his arm. "I'm kidding you."

"Lobster?" Evan extended his plate toward her.

"At least you know how to bribe me." She snatched a lobster piece and popped it in her mouth. "I never turn down food."

"You two do make a cute couple," Divya said. "Particularly as spies."

"And you are a gorgeous colonial lady," Evan said.

My brother the charmer.

"Why, thank you, Mr. Lawson." Divya gave a curtsy.

"My pleasure, Ms. Katdare." Evan bowed slightly.

"As much as we're enjoying this little mutual admiration society," I said, "we're going to go mingle."

"Count me in," Divya said.

Jill, Divya, and I moved into the crowd, where we ran into the Shanahans. We chatted for a few minutes and then made our way out to the rear patio. The sun was giving the western horizon her final brushstrokes and a soft, warm breeze came off the calm ocean.

"I could live here," Jill said.

"Who couldn't?" I slid my arm around her. "Want me to buy it for you?"

Divya laughed.

Jill said, "You wish."

"Who knows? Maybe someday."

Now Jill laughed. "Dream on. HankMed might be successful, but it will never be this successful."

"You're hurting my feelings. I might cry."

She looked at me. "This I want to see."

"Maybe not cry, but my feelings are still hurt."

"A dose of reality does that to you sometimes," Divya said.

"You wouldn't be happy here anyway," Jill said.

"I wouldn't?"

"It's way too un-Hank."

"Un-Hank?"

"Too ostentatious."

She had a point. I had no idea what this place cost, but I'm sure it was staggering. Like many other properties in the area. The value of some equaled the GDP of more than a few countries. Not that I didn't enjoy living at Shadow Pond, a mansion that was probably worth two or three Nathan Zimmer estates, but I'm not sure I'd want to own it.

Then again, who was I kidding?

"Hank, how are you?"

I turned. It was Nathan. We shook hands.

"Divya." He shook her hand.

I introduced him to Jill.

"Ah, Ms. Casey. The brains behind Hamptons Heritage."

"Don't know that I'd say that," Jill said.

"From what I hear it's an accurate assessment."

Even in the dim light I could see Jill blushing. "That's very kind of you to say."

"Are you having fun?" Nathan asked.

"Very much," Jill said.

"Love the way you've decorated everything," Divya said.

"You don't think it's too much?"

"Not at all. It's breathtaking."

"As is this view," I said.

Nathan gazed out toward the ocean and nodded. "That's the main reason I bought this place." He looked back toward us. "That's why I work from here most days. No place I'd rather be."

"Yeah," Jill said, "I was just thinking how much this place reminds me of my apartment."

Nathan laughed. "It is a bit much, isn't it?" He looked toward the house. "And a bit much to keep up with sometimes. Most of the rooms sit empty."

"I'm available for adoption," Jill said.

Nathan laughed again. "I never knew hospital administrators were so funny."

"Most aren't," I said. "At least not the ones I've known."

"You're not thinking of one in particular, are you?" Nathan asked.

I shrugged.

"Raw deal," Nathan continued. "No doubt about it."

I agreed.

Nathan took a sip from the glass he held. "Soda water. See, I do listen."

"Maybe you should talk to some of our other patients," Divya said. "The ones that don't listen so well."

"Speaking of other patients," Nathan said, "I stopped by and saw Jimmy Sutter. He looked amazingly good for what he's been through."

"He's a tough guy," I said.

"And a good man," Nathan said. "Done work for me for years."

Someone called Nathan's name from the other end of the patio. I looked that way. Two attractive women waved to him. Both wore ball gowns, one soft pink, the other dark green.

"Excuse me," Nathan said. "My fans await."

"No problem," I said. "We'll chat later."

Nathan walked to where the two women stood. Hugs and kisses followed. Todd, Nathan's assistant, appeared behind him, whispered something to Nathan, and then retreated back into the house. Nathan hooked arms with the two women and they all followed Todd.

"Fans, huh?" Jill asked.

"I'd suspect a bachelor with Nathan's bank account has a waiting list of fans."

"Waiting list?" Jill asked.

"More applicants for the position than he can handle."

"And what position might that be?" Divya said, an eyebrow arched in my direction.

Uh-oh. My brain searched for a clever answer. The first thought was "all of them," but I tucked that one away. What, then? Divya crossed her arms as if saying, "Well, we're waiting."

"Here he is."

It was Evan, standing in the rear doorway, his cane aimed in my direction.

There are things you never want to hear come from Evan's mouth. Things like, "I have a great idea," or "I need to talk to you," or as in this case, "Here he is." Nothing good ever follows such pronouncements. At least he distracted Divya and Jill, as both turned to look at him.

Turned out this "here he is" wasn't bad at all. Evan led Eleanor Louise Parker Wentworth through the door and toward us. Ellie—to her friends, and to me—is one of my favorite patients. She looked magnificent in a colonial ball gown.

"You look great," I said.

"You're just saying that."

"I'm saying it because it's true."

"You do," Jill said. Divya agreed.

"It's so lovely to see all of you," Ellie said. "It's been a while."

"The wedding," Jill said.

Ellie, known for her outlandishly prefect parties, had thrown a huge one for her granddaughter's wedding. Which almost didn't happen. Granddaughter Nicole had a few "spells" that put the entire wedding in jeopardy. Until Divya and I uncovered that these spells were actually temporal lobe epilepsy. A few meds and Nicole was a picture-perfect bride.

"How is Nicole?" I asked.

"Marvelous. They had a wonderful honeymoon and are now back to the real world and building a life together in the city."

The music faded and people began to pour out of the house and onto the patio. Todd, dressed as the town crier, led the way, stopping at the edge of the patio and turning back to face the gathering.

"It's time for the fireworks," Todd announced. "You can easily see them from here, but if you want to get up close we'll go down to the beach and watch."

Nathan reappeared, flanked by the two women I had seen earlier. He descended the steps and, like the Pied Piper, led maybe two-thirds of the guests across the lawn toward the sand. Evan and Danielle decided to stay on the patio with Angela, who said the walk was a bit far for her. Ellie said she'd stay on the deck, too. Divya agreed. Jill and I joined the group headed for the front row.

It must have been a hundred yards down to the boundary of Nathan's estate. Jill and I moved to the right side, where we had a clear view of the water yet were free of the crowd.

The first rocket sizzled skyward and exploded in a huge red, white, and blue scintillating ball. Oohs and aahs followed. As did more fireworks.

"Take off your shoes," I said.

"Why?"

"To go for a walk on the beach."

"And miss the fireworks?"

"We can see them from there."

"You're on."

And that's what we did. Leaving our shoes on the grass, we crossed the sand to where the water lapped at it, making it firm and cool. We stood watching explosion after explosion light up the night sky, flash kaleidoscopic colors across the upturned faces of the crowd, and paint broken reflections on the water. I curled my arm around Jill and she rested her head against my shoulder.

Life was good.

Funny how that is. A few years ago I had lost my job and had no future and now here I was standing with the Hamptons elite on the estate of one of the richest men in the world, with a group of people I wouldn't have known or even thought I wanted to know, back then. People who I had always assumed were too rich to be real.

Amazing how all that had changed. These were people just like everyone else. Sure, they had more money than most could imagine, but they had the same problems as the rest of us. How do you raise your children? How do you keep life fun and interesting? How do you deal with tragedy? How do you find happiness?

Universally human problems. They don't have social boundaries.

Even better, here I stood, enjoying this evening with someone I care about and who I know cares about me.

Why weren't we together? Really together? I'm not sure, but the closest I could come to a rational explanation was that neither of us was ready for a stronger commitment. Someday maybe, hopefully, but not just yet.

Still, life was good.

Also available in the new series
based on the hit USA Network
television show!

ROYAL PAINS
First, Do No Harm

by D. P. Lyle

Hamptons aristocrat Eleanor Parker Wentworth is one of
HankMed's most cherished patients. With her granddaughter's
wedding coming up, Ms. Wentworth is quite stressed.

But Hank is more concerned with the bride-to-be, Nicole.
After Hank meets her at a prewedding party, she shows no
recognition of him later that same night. Is it a case of wedding-
day jitters—or of something much more serious? With a
high-end guest list waiting for the walk down the aisle, Hank
will have to think fast and work faster before the wedding
march turns into a funeral dirge...

**Available wherever books are sold or at
penguin.com**

OM0059

Searching for the perfect mystery?

Looking for a place to get the latest clues and connect with fellow fans?

"Like" The Crime Scene on Facebook!

- Participate in author chats
- Enter book giveaways
- Learn about the latest releases
- Get book recommendations
- Send mystery-themed gifts to friends and more!

facebook.com/TheCrimeSceneBooks

Obsidian